This season Harlequin® Romance brings you

Christmas Treats

For an extra-special treat this Christmas
don't look under the Christmas tree or in
your stocking—pick up one of your favorite
Harlequin Romance novels, curl up and relax!

From presents to proposals, mistletoe to marriage,
we promise to deliver seasonal warmth, wonder
and of course the unbeatable rush of romance!

*And look out for Christmas surprises
this month in Harlequin Romance!*

"Okay, Cullen!" Harry said, handing him a cookie. *"You paint this one. It's a bell."*

"I see that."

"So paint it."

"With frosting," Wendy qualified. "But you should also wash your hands first."

He was going to say no. He'd never done anything like this in his life and he was too old to start now. But just the mention of the word *frosting* squeezed his heart. Unable to catch every word said about him, Harry had repeated what he'd thought he heard and called himself a "frosting child." He was a sweet little boy, left in the hands of a cold, sterile system. How could Cullen turn down the request of a child who'd just lost his mother?

"Okay."

Wendy smiled. Cullen's heart tripped over itself in his chest. Now that they were in a comfortable environment he'd begun thinking of things a little more normally. But that wasn't necessarily good. Instead of envisioning off-the-wall images like sparkling angels when he looked at her, he was now thinking how he'd like to kiss the lips that had pulled upward into a smile.

But that was wrong. They'd be working together in the weeks to come. Visions of angels were one thing. Actually wanting to kiss his temporary employee was another.

SUSAN MEIER
The Magic of a Family Christmas

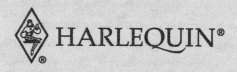

TORONTO • NEW YORK • LONDON
AMSTERDAM • PARIS • SYDNEY • HAMBURG
STOCKHOLM • ATHENS • TOKYO • MILAN • MADRID
PRAGUE • WARSAW • BUDAPEST • AUCKLAND

Recycling programs
for this product may
not exist in your area.

ISBN-13: 978-0-373-17622-9

THE MAGIC OF A FAMILY CHRISTMAS

First North American Publication 2009.

Susan Meier spent most of her twenties thinking she was a job-hopper—until she began to write and realized everything that had come before was only research! As one of eleven children, with twenty-four nieces and nephews and three kids of her own, Susan has had plenty of real-life experience watching romance blossom in unexpected ways. She lives in Western Pennsylvania with her wonderful husband, Mike, three children and two overfed, well-cuddled cats, Sophie and Fluffy. You can visit Susan's Web site at www.susanmeier.com.

PROLOGUE

"I've hired a nurse."

"Really?" Wendy Winston tried to sound surprised by her next-door neighbor's announcement, but she wasn't. Betsy's cancer hadn't responded to treatment. Wendy had been able to help Betsy struggle through the aftereffects of the initial round of chemotherapy, but her friend needed real care now. Care beyond what a neighbor could provide.

"I appreciate all the help you've given me over the past few weeks, but I'll bet you'll be glad for the break."

Fluffing the fat pillow before she slid it under Betsy's head, Wendy laughed. "You think I'll be glad to go back to an empty house?"

Betsy frowned. "I've always wondered why you didn't move back to your family in Ohio after your husband died."

She shrugged. "Memories mostly. It seemed too abrupt just to leave when he died. I needed time to process everything."

"It's been two years."

"I also have a job."

"No one stays away from family for a job."

She grinned at Betsy. "Would you believe I can't sell that monstrosity I call a house?"

Betsy laughed.

"One of these days I'll have the kitchen and bathrooms re-modeled and then I can put it on the market and go."

Even Wendy heard the wistfulness in her own voice so she wasn't surprised when Betsy said, "It makes you sad to think of leaving."

"Four years ago I settled here with the assumption that Barrington would be my home. I can't shake the feeling that this is where I belong. No matter how alone I am."

"Why didn't you and Greg ever have kids?"

"He wanted to be done with his residency before we even tried."

"Makes sense."

Wendy smiled sadly.

"But it didn't make you happy."

"If we'd done what I wanted and had a child I wouldn't be alone right now." She sighed. "Not that I only wanted a child to keep from being lonely. It was more than that. My whole life I longed to be a mom. But what Greg wanted always came first. Some days I struggle with that."

"That's one of those tough choices that happens in a marriage. Nobody's fault."

Wendy turned away. "Yeah." She wouldn't burden Betsy with stories of how her late husband had been so focused and determined that he frequently didn't even listen when she talked. She didn't want to give Betsy any more to worry about or the wrong idea. She had loved Greg and missed him so much after he died that she had genuinely believed she would never be happy again. But because he was so self-absorbed, their marriage was far from perfect.

Silence stretched out in Betsy's sunny bedroom as Wendy walked around the room tidying the dresser and bedside tables.

"You know, it won't be the nurse's job to read Harry a story or tuck him in at night," Betsy said, referring to her six-year-old son.

Wendy turned from the dresser.

"So if you want to keep coming over to do that, I know it would make Harry happy. He loves it when you read to him."

Wendy smiled. "I love it, too."

CHAPTER ONE

WENDY Winston twisted the key to silence her small car and turned to the boy on the seat beside her. Six-year-old Harry Martin blinked at her from behind brown-framed glasses. A knit cap covered his short yellow hair. His blue eyes were far too serious to be those of a child. A thick winter coat swallowed his thin body. His mittened hand clutched a bag of toy soldiers.

"I'm really sorry to have to bring you to work."

He pushed his glasses up his nose. "S'okay."

She wanted to say not really. It wasn't okay that he'd be forced to sit and play with his plastic soldiers for God only knew how long while she worked. It wasn't okay that he'd lost his mom. Or that Betsy's lawyer had been out of town when she'd died. It had been four weeks before Attorney Costello had finally called to tell Wendy that Betsy had granted her custody of Harry in her will, and another few days before social services could pull him out of his foster home and give Wendy custody—and then only temporarily.

Regardless of what Betsy's will said, Harry's biological father's rights superseded her custody bequest. But no one knew where Harry's dad was, so, for now, Wendy had a child who needed her, and, for the first time in two years, she had someone to anticipate Christmas with. Though social services was searching for Harry's dad, Wendy believed she and Harry could have as long as a month to shop, bake cookies and decorate. If it killed her she would make it the best month before Christmas this little boy had ever had.

She smiled. "I promise I'll make this up to you."

"Can we bake cookies?"

Her heart soared. It seemed that what he needed done for him was what she needed to do. They were the perfect combination. Maybe fate wasn't so despicable after all.

"You bet we can bake cookies. Any kind you want."

Wicked wind battered them with freezing rain as they raced across the icy parking lot to the executive entrance for Barrington Candies. Juggling her umbrella and her purse as they ran toward the door, she rummaged for her key, but before she found it, the right side of the glass double doors burst open.

Cullen Barrington stood in the entryway. Six foot three, with black hair and eyes every bit as dark, and wearing a pale-blue sweater that was probably cashmere, the owner of Barrington Candies was the consummate playboy. He was rich, handsome and rarely around, assigning her boss Paul McCoy the task of managing the day-to-day operations of the company while he handled the big-picture details from the comfort of his home in Miami. Cullen was also so tight with money that no one in the plant had gotten a raise since control of Barrington Candies had been handed to him by his mother.

Scrooge.

That's what she'd taken to calling the man who'd summoned her to work on a Saturday afternoon. Even though he'd surprised everyone with his offer to fill in for her boss so Mr. McCoy could take an extended Christmas vacation,

Wendy wasn't fooled into thinking he'd changed his ways and become generous. Though he'd probably called her in today to prepare before he took over on Monday morning, he'd paid no thought to the fact that she would lose her day off. She'd lose precious minutes with Harry. She'd lose the chance for them to enjoy whatever time they had together, and maybe even the chance for her to show him life wasn't entirely bad, just parts of it.

Even if, some days, she didn't quite believe that herself.

Occupied with her thoughts, she slipped on the ice and plowed into Cullen. She braced her hand on his chest to stop her forward momentum and it sank into the downy cashmere covering the hard muscle of his chest. His body was like a rock.

Confused, because she thought all rich men were soft and pampered, she looked up. He glanced down. And everything inside Wendy stilled. She swore the world stopped revolving. As dark as moonless midnight, his eyes held hers. Her femininity stirred inside her.

That confused her even more. She hadn't felt anything for a man since her husband's death, and Cullen Barrington was the last man on the planet she wanted to be attracted to. A playboy from Miami? No thanks. She'd glimpsed him a time or two in the four years she'd been working for his company and never felt anything but distaste at the way he treated his employees. She had no idea what was going on with her hormones, but it had to be an aberration of some sort.

She stepped away, and as the door swung closed behind her a bell rang.

Funny, she didn't remember a bell being on that door.

She turned to investigate and sure enough someone had tied a bell to the spring mechanism at the top of the door.

Probably Wendell, the janitor, making sure he'd be alerted if one of the executives sneaked in to check up on him.

"Why did you bring your little boy?"

She pulled off her mittens. "Oh, I don't know. Because I wasn't supposed to be working today? Because it's such short notice that I couldn't get a sitter?" She shrugged. "Take your pick."

His gorgeous eyes narrowed. He obviously didn't like her speaking so freely with him.

Wendy almost groaned at her stupidity. A single woman who might get custody of a little boy couldn't afford to be fired!

"I'm sorry. I shouldn't have snapped at you. It's just cold and I had things to do. So tell me what you want to work on and we can get started."

"I'd like to catch up on what's been going on, so I'll need production schedules and the financials. Once you help me find those, you can go home."

He didn't smile. Didn't give any reason at all for her heart to catch at the smooth baritone of his voice, but it did. Her entire body felt warm and soft, feminine in response to his masculinity.

She stepped back. She did not want to be attracted to him. It had taken her two long, miserable years to get over Greg's death. And she refused to go through the misery of loss again by being attracted to a playboy who—as sure as the sun rises every day—would dump her.

Of course, she might not be attracted to Cullen as much as she was simply waking up from the sexual dead. It *had* been two years. And she had been feeling like her normal self for at least three months. Maybe this was just a stage?

She peeked at Cullen, knowing that beneath that soft sweater was a very hard male body. Something sweet and syrupy floated through her. Moving her gaze upward, she met his simmering dark eyes and knew she could get lost in them.

She swallowed. Nope. Not a stage. It was him. She was attracted to *him*.

He turned to walk back to the office. Following him, she caught Harry's hand and brought him along with her.

"As far as the financials go, I don't want those fancy reports that go out in the annual statement. I want the spreadsheets. The nuts and bolts."

She stopped with a frown. She had access to everything, but if he was looking for the whys behind the line entries, she couldn't help him. "Why didn't you call Nolan, the accountant?"

He faced her. "Are you saying you can't get me the financials?"

"No. I have them. Everything is in my filing cabinet. But—"

She stopped talking. First, his eyes were simmering sexily again and her whole body began to hum—which made her want to groan in frustration. Second, she was making this harder than it had to be. All she had to do was find a few documents for him. The faster she found them, the sooner she'd be at home making cookies.

She squeezed Harry's hand. "I can get you anything you need."

"Thank you."

Cullen turned and resumed his walk to the executive suite. Wendy and Harry scurried behind him.

In her office, she stripped off her coat and removed Harry's. Cullen stood patiently by her desk as she rummaged through her purse for the key to the filing cabinet. Walking over, she noticed the door to her boss's office was open. Papers were strewn across his desk.

"Oh, you're already working?"

Cullen nodded. "I typed a few letters. But there isn't a printer in the office. I'm guessing I have to send my things to a remote printer, but I'm not sure which one is which."

"E-mail them to me and I'll print them."

"Why don't you just come to the computer with me and show me which printer to send them to?"

Okay. So he didn't want her to see what he'd written. No big deal. Whatever he wanted to print was probably personal. Not her business. She not only got the message; she also agreed. The less she knew about this man and the faster she got away from him, the better.

She unlocked the cabinet, pulled out the accordion file that contained the backup documentation for the financials for the year that had passed and handed it to him.

He glanced at the packet, then back up at her. Her stomach flip-flopped. His eyes were incredible. Dark. Shiny. Sexy. And the perfect complement to his angular face. He had the look of a matador. Strong. Bold. Everything about him was dramatic, male.

"Is the forecast in here?"

With a quick shake of her head, she rid herself of those ridiculous thoughts, not sure where the heck they kept coming from but knowing they were absolutely wrong. She returned her attention to the open drawer and pulled the file folder for the five-year plan. "Here you go."

"Great."

Cullen took the folder from her hands and stepped back. He'd thought that bringing in Paul's administrative assistant would make his life easier, but this woman wasn't at all what he'd been expecting. For a widow, she was young and incredibly good-looking. Long, loosely curled red hair fell to the shoulders of her thick green cable-knit sweater. Her cheeks had become pink in the cold, accenting the green of her eyes. Low-riding jeans hugged a shapely bottom.

He wasn't sure what the heck had happened when she'd fallen into his arms after she'd slipped on the ice. Their eyes had met and he'd felt a jolt of something so foreign it had rendered him speechless. He couldn't blame it on the fact that she was attractive. He knew hundreds of gorgeous women. Women even prettier than she was. He couldn't say it was because she was sexy. He knew sexy women. And he couldn't say he'd felt a jolt because he was happy to see her. He didn't know her.

But whatever the hell that jolt was, he was smart enough to ignore it.

He was also taking that damned bell off the door. The whole point of having an executive entry was so the workers didn't know when he was there or he wasn't!

"Come on. Show me how to send these letters to a remote printer."

She followed him into the office of the current company president and her little boy followed her.

"What's your name?"

"Harry."

Cullen couldn't help it; he laughed. "Like Harry Potter?"

"No, like my grandpa."

He turned to Wendy Winston. "So your father was a Harry?"

"No, *his* grandfather's name was Harry."

Confused, Cullen stopped and faced them again. He looked from Wendy to Harry and back to Wendy again. They didn't look a thing alike. So the kid probably resembled his dad which meant that Grandpa Harry had been her late husband's dad. Whatever the deal, he really didn't care. He was trying to make light conversation so the afternoon would go more smoothly. If they wanted to play guessing games, he wasn't interested.

He turned and walked behind the desk, falling into the uncomfortable desk chair. With a few keystrokes he minimized his letters and left a blank screen. He rose and motioned for Wendy to take a seat in the chair.

"Show me which printer to send these to."

She sat. "Okay. Well, you just do all the things you need to do to print—" Using the mouse, she clicked the appropriate icon to get the print menu.

When the print menu popped on the screen, he leaned down to get a closer look. The scent of something floral drifted to his nose. With a slight movement of his eyes, he took in her shiny red hair—more the color of cinnamon than autumn leaves—then let his gaze drift down to her shapely breasts.

Damn it! Why did he keep looking at her?

"Once you get this screen, you scroll to the top, click this menu to get the available printers, and choose this printer. Your documents will be sent to the printer by my desk."

He cleared his throat. "Okay. I get it. Thank you. You can go now."

She rose from the desk chair and caught Harry's hand. "I can leave?"

"Yes. All I wanted were the financials and production reports, and to know which printer was closest." He plopped down on the chair again and she turned to go but another thought struck him. "Wait!"

She faced him.

"You aren't leaving town, are you?"

She laughed and he frowned. The last review in the personnel file for Wendy Winston had described her as quiet and unassuming, but extremely capable. He'd never know that from her behavior today. Of course, the way he kept staring at her, his attention continually caught by parts of her body he normally wouldn't look at with an employee, wasn't normal either. All because she'd fallen into his arms.

So maybe that brush had affected her as much as him? And maybe he should just ignore the way she was acting?

After a few seconds of silence, she gasped. "Oh, you weren't kidding about my leaving town?"

"Why did you think I was kidding? Everybody else in this company is out of town."

She gaped at him. "Because it's the holiday! People are going to parties and visiting friends and relatives for Thanksgiving!"

"Right." Because his holiday had been uneventful he'd almost forgotten it altogether. He looked down at his papers, then back up at her. "I'm not Scrooge. I'm just trying to make sure I don't lose my source for information."

She pulled in a breath. Her breasts rose and fell. Realizing he was staring, he jerked his eyes upward, cursing himself for acting like a horny teenager.

"No, Harry and I are staying in town. Even weekends."

"Great." Forcing his mind off her sweater and to the mission he was here to accomplish, he rubbed his hands together over the keyboard. "I'll call you if I need you."

She turned and left the office. Though Cullen had thought his attention was on the family business, where it was supposed to be, he couldn't resist glancing up to watch the sway of her hips as she left.

Because her back was to him, he braced his elbow on his desk and his chin on his closed fist, letting himself watch as he tried to figure this out. He felt bewitched. But he couldn't be. They hadn't spent more than ten minutes together. And she wasn't his type. He liked blondes. And she was a widow. A serious woman, not to be trifled with.

So he wouldn't trifle. He would be the perfect gentleman for the few weeks he had to run this company, and then he'd leave Barrington, Pennsylvania, and, he hoped, never again even set foot in the town that bore his family's name.

Wendy hustled Harry into the foyer of her echoing home. Her house was a monstrosity, a five-bedroom, three-bath mansion built in the eighteen hundreds that had been updated with the times, but had gone into disrepair when the last owner had left town and let it sit empty for over a year. She and her husband had purchased it with the idea of turning it into their dream home. They'd gotten as far as ripping out carpeting and finishing the hardwood floors throughout the house, chucking wood paneling in favor of plastered walls and installing a new furnace, roof and windows. But Greg had died before they even touched the bathrooms or the kitchen, which could best be described as early-American. As in Revolutionary War.

She turned up the thermostat to accommodate the howling wind outside and pointed Harry in the direction of the kitchen.

Creamsicle, her fat orange-and-white cat, thumped down the stairs and wrapped himself around her legs in greeting.

She motioned to the cat, diverting Harry's attention to him. "Harry, this is Creamsicle. Creamsicle, this is Harry."

The cat blinked. Harry grinned. "You have a cat!"

"Yes, but he's old and moody, so you have to be nice to him." She stooped down to pet Creamsicle, who ignored Harry—which was probably for the best. "I seem to remember something about Christmas cookies."

Harry's eyes grew as big as her cat's belly. "Can we make them red and green?"

She began walking to the kitchen. "Hey, if you want to paint stained-glass windows on the church cookies, that's fine by me."

"We're making churches?"

"I have a cutter for a church. One for Santa. An angel."

She walked to the cabinet by the refrigerator. Her cupboards were knotty pine that actually made her dizzy. Especially when combined with the green-and-white print in the linoleum floor. She'd replaced the busy leaf-print curtains with simple taupe panels, removed the floral wallpaper and painted the walls a soothing sage color. But she hadn't been able to replace the cabinets or the floor and the floor/cabinet combo sometimes gave her motion sickness.

"Here's a bell, a wreath, a Christmas tree," she said, pulling the cookie cutters from the deep drawer. "Let me grab the ingredients for the cookies and we'll get this show on the road."

"Don't you think I should take off my coat first?"

She laughed, walking toward him, as Creamsicle waddled in and took his place on the floor in the corner, watching her and the newcomer.

"I don't have any kids so I'm going to forget some obvious things every once in a while." She unzipped his coat and tugged on the sleeve to pull it off then yanked his cap off his head. "Don't be afraid to remind me!"

"Okay." He pushed his glasses up his nose.

After stowing his coat and hat in the hall closet, Wendy gathered sugar, vanilla and flour from the cupboards and eggs, butter and milk from the refrigerator. Harry climbed on a chair.

"Oh, no! No sitting for you! You have to help."

He peeked up at her. "Really?"

"Sure." She handed him a measuring cup. "Fill that with flour."

Standing on the chair, he peered into the canister, then back at her. "Fill it?"

"Just dip it in." She cupped his soft little hand over the handle of the measuring cup and scooped it into the flour to fill it. "See? Like that."

"Cool!"

"I'm guessing you've never baked before."

He shook his head. "My mom didn't have time."

Wendy nearly cursed at her stupid mistake. The last thing she wanted to do was remind him of his mother, but before she had a chance to say anything, the phone rang.

Wendy walked to the wall unit talking. "You never having baked isn't a big deal. In fact, it will be fun for me to teach you. Something new for both of us." She lifted the phone receiver. "Hello?"

"This isn't the right forecast."

"Oh, hello, Mr. Barrington."

"This forecast has *draft* written on it. Every copy in the file has *draft* stamped on it. Isn't there a final version?"

"Yes." She thought for a second, wondering why her final copy wasn't in the file, but in the end decided it didn't matter. "I probably have to print you another copy."

"Great. I'll see you when you get here." He paused then added, "And don't dillydally."

He hung up the phone.

She sighed. "Harry, do me a favor and put the butter back in the fridge."

He scooted off the chair and took the butter to the refrigerator. Right behind him with the milk and eggs, Wendy caught the door as he opened it.

"This is so much fun!"

She frowned. "Getting things out and putting them away again is fun?"

"Having somewhere to go!"

"You like going to work?"

"I like going *anywhere*. My mom didn't go places." He frowned then glanced at the floor. "She was sick."

Wendy stooped down in front of him. Her own pang of loss rippled through her as she remembered Betsy. "I know she was sick. And I'll bet you miss her. But I don't think she'd want you dwelling on her."

"What's dwelling?"

"Thinking about her when she can't be here. I'll bet she'd want you to think happy thoughts this close to Christmas."

Even as the words came out of her mouth they brought a rush of memory. Her mom had told her the same thing about Greg. That she shouldn't dwell on him, their plans, their life. She remembered thinking that her mom was right and still being angry that he'd died, had left her when she'd loved him so much, needed him so much. Two years without him had taught her to be stronger, bolder and independent enough never to fall into the trap of needing a man the way she had Greg. But when her mom had said those words, she'd been devastated.

Harry, however, nodded sagely.

She rose and helped him with his coat. After shrugging into her own coat and getting her purse and keys from the table in the foyer, she caught Harry's hand and led him outside into the driving wind and freezing rain.

Ice now covered tree branches and clung to the mailboxes of the row of older, but well-tended homes. She paused in front of her little blue car, studying the icicles that hung from the door handle. It was so easy for a car to slide on ice. Walking might be safer. "I'm not sure about this."

"About what?"

"The plant isn't very far from here. We could actually walk."

But it was raining. And Harry was a little boy. A simple ten-minute walk for her might not be so easy for short legs.

She frowned. "Never mind. We'll drive."

As they waited for the car windows to defrost, she said, "So do you know what you want to be when you grow up?"

"A fireman."

"That's a great job."

"I want to save people."

Wendy yanked her gearshift out of Park and into Drive. With his mother's passing so fresh in his memory, there was no way Wendy would let him go down that road. Not this close to Christmas. If nothing else, she intended to give this little boy a break from reality. A few days or weeks of comfort and joy while social services employees hunted for his dad.

"Maybe if you're good enough with the cookies, you might want to consider being a baker."

He giggled. "Girls are bakers."

"Not really." As they drove to the plant, they talked about the different kinds of jobs he could consider then she took his hand again to help him navigate the icy parking lot. This time she needed her key to get in.

When they arrived in her office, Cullen Barrington was standing by her desk, looking at his watch.

"Five minutes? I told you to hurry, but I didn't mean for you to be reckless."

"I wasn't. I don't live far." She rubbed her hands together before removing her coat. "We actually considered walking, but it's freezing out there."

"If you think you're cold, you should be me. In Miami the temperature rarely falls below sixty. I'm lucky that I remembered to bring a winter coat. Even with it I shiver."

He was trying to make small talk, to be nice, she supposed, to take the sting out of calling her into the office again, and she smiled at him. He returned her smile and her nerve endings shimmered with life and energy, even as her brain filled with silly, romantic notions. Maybe this incredibly handsome man wasn't a Scrooge after all? Maybe beneath that playboy exterior was a nice guy? Then all these feelings she had of drowning in his dark eyes wouldn't be wrong. Maybe she'd get to kiss that mouth, be held in his strong arms—

Luckily, he had turned and didn't see her shaking her head to clear those thoughts. They were ridiculous! Even thinking about getting involved with someone like him was dangerous. He probably practiced being nice to seduce unsuspecting females like her! She needed to keep her feet firmly grounded in her real world. She was strong now, independent, not dreamy as she had been when she'd fallen for Greg. Cullen needed one little thing printed, the forecast, then she and Harry could go home and bake.

She slid onto her desk chair, turned on her computer, hit a few keystrokes and the room went dark.

CHAPTER TWO

"WHAT did you do?"

So much for thinking that deep down inside he was a nice guy. "I didn't do anything!"

A childish whimper floated to Wendy. Her office didn't have a window, so when the lights went out, the room became pitch-black.

She bounced from her seat. "Harry, everything's fine. The ice probably brought down a power line or two."

"Damn."

That had been Cullen.

Sliding her fingers across the edge of her desk, she began feeling her way to Harry. Instead, she bumped into Cullen's thighs. Once again solid muscle greeted her and she jerked her hands away. It seemed fate was determined to find ways for her to touch him.

"Sorry!"

He cleared his throat. "It's fine. I think Harry's about two paces to your left."

She found her way to Harry. Putting her hand on his shoulder for security, she said, "Here's what we'll do. It's still light outside, so we can open the drapes in Mr. McCoy's office." She squeezed the little boy's shoulder. "Is it okay for me to go and do that?"

Harry said, "Yes."

"Okay. You stay here." She carefully navigated past her desk, praying Cullen hadn't moved in the thirty seconds she'd spoken with Harry.

"Don't you have a flashlight or something?"

Cullen's voice came from behind her, thank God.

"I'm sure there's one in maintenance. Would you like to walk through the dark plant and then down the dark-as-night steps to the basement to get it?"

"Very funny."

In another few seconds she found her boss's desk and walked to the window behind it. Running her hands along the curtain, she found the pull string and opened the drapes. Pale light filtered in, but it was enough that she could see Harry and Cullen.

"If you guys want to sit in here, I'll—"

Before she finished her sentence, Harry raced into the office. She stooped and caught him as he threw himself at her. "Are you okay?"

"Yeah," he said, but he hugged her fiercely.

Looking away, Cullen scrubbed his hand across his mouth. "Now, what do we do?"

"It depends on how long it takes for the electricity to come back on." She rose and grabbed Harry's hand. "Benny Owens works just inside the door to the plant. He has a radio. It runs on batteries. It's a mandate of our safety manual because in an emergency, we can tune it to the local station and hear what's going on. There are five of them in strategic locations throughout the building. Benny's is the closest."

"Makes sense."

"I'm the most familiar with the plant layout so I'll go and get the radio." She stooped in front of Harry. "Do you want to stay here with Mr. Barrington or come with me?"

He glanced at Cullen, then back at her, pulled in a big breath and said, "I'll keep an eye on him."

Wendy laughed, rose and tousled his hair. The kid certainly caught on fast. "This should only take about five minutes."

Standing in the semi-dark room with the uncomfortable little boy who'd promised to keep an eye on him, Cullen frowned. One minute turned into two. Two turned into three. Harry began to squirm.

"Don't worry. Your mom will be back soon."

The little boy peered up at him. "She's not my mom."

"Your aunt?"

He shook his head. "She's nothing."

Cullen frowned. "Nothing?"

Harry pushed his glasses up his nose. "I'm a frosting child."

"A *frosting* child?"

"You know. Somebody else has to take care of me until portal services decides what to do with me."

"Portal services?"

Exasperated, Harry said, "The place that puts kids in a home."

"Oh! *Social services*. You're a *foster* kid."

He nodded. "Yeah. My mom died."

Cullen's heart stopped. Sadness filled him. Hoping he'd heard wrong, he said, "Your mom died?"

He nodded again.

Cullen bent down to talk to Harry on his own level. "Mine did, too."

"Really?"

"A few months ago. January." He shook his head in wonder. Time had certainly flown. "It's been almost a year, but I still miss her."

"I miss my mom, too." He caught Cullen's gaze. "She was sick though. Everybody says she's happy now."

Cullen nearly cursed. At the wake when people had told him his mother was in a better place, he'd believed it. But it was cruel to tell this little boy his mom preferred leaving him to staying with him.

"I'm guessing you don't have any aunts or uncles?"

He shook his head.

Though he hesitated, half afraid of the answer, Cullen asked, "Where's your dad?"

Harry shrugged. "He's around somewhere." Then he flapped his arms in exasperation, as if this is what he'd seen and heard adults do when they talked about his dad. "We'll find him eventually."

The kid was just a tad too observant.

The light from the window in Mr. McCoy's office thinned as Wendy walked farther into the building, but when she reached the main corridor, emergency lights were lit. She scrambled to the door and into the plant. At Benny Owens's workstation, she snatched the radio and quickly made her way back to Cullen and Harry.

The second she stepped into the office, Cullen caught her gaze. His normally bright eyes were soft, sincere.

"Harry was telling me about his mom."

"Oh." She glanced at Harry, who looked up at her with a smile. "You okay, little guy?"

Still smiling, he nodded.

Whatever had happened between the two of them, Harry was okay. He might have even gotten afraid in the dark again and Cullen had taken care of him. Surprising, but good. She turned to smile at Cullen in thanks, but when their gazes caught, that funny feeling happened in her stomach again. Only this time, her chest also tightened. It became hard to breathe. She sort of felt as if she were drowning in the deep pools of his eyes, once again overwhelmed by the strange instinct that deep down he really was a nice guy—

The church bell across the street rang twice, jolting her back to reality.

"Must be two o'clock," she said, brightly, trying to pretend nothing *had* happened because nothing had happened. So they'd looked into each other's eyes? It wasn't a big deal.

Setting the radio on her boss's desk, she said, "I forgot about the emergency lights. The corridors are well-lit. The plant has emergency lighting, too."

She turned on the radio and slowly moved the dial until she found the local station. The announcer said, "The mayor is telling everybody to just sit tight—"

She glanced at Cullen. "Either I have perfect timing or this is an emergency broadcast that's repeating."

"To repeat… Trees and power lines are down all over town. Route 81 has been shut down due to accidents."

Cullen cursed.

She faced him. "What?"

"That's the only highway out of town. The only way to get to my hotel."

"I'm sure it will be open before you want to go back."

"Since I can't work without a computer, I want to go back now."

"Good point."

They both glanced at the radio.

"I'm sorry to say, folks," the announcer said, "the power

company is warning that this is going to be an all-nighter. Get out your candles, light your fireplace, and be careful."

The announcer stopped talking and a song floated from the radio. Wendy shifted away from the desk. Technically, she and Harry could leave. They could even bake their cookies. She had a gas stove. And a fireplace. They could roast marshmallows and sleep in sleeping bags on the living-room floor.

This could actually be the most fun day of his stay with her.

She put her hand on Harry's shoulder, took another step back, easing toward the door.

It almost seemed wrong to leave. Almost. The truth was she didn't know Cullen Barrington. And she was attracted to him. The first man since Greg. That left her feeling odd enough. When she added that he was a playboy, out of her reach, the man who owned the company she worked for, in front of whom she'd prefer to be on her best behavior, not walking around a dark old house with a flashlight… Well, it was for the best that she not invite him to her home. She shouldn't feel guilty for leaving him to figure out what he'd do for the next twelve to twenty-four hours—in the dark—when she not only had light and warmth, she could also cook dinner.

While he sat in the dark? Slept on the floor with his jacket for a cover?

Damn it!

Why couldn't her conscience just shut up long enough for her to get to her car?

"Do you want to come with us?"

His head jerked up. "Where are you going?"

"As you said, we can't work in the dark. So Harry and I are going home. I have a gas stove and a working fireplace in the living room. Even my hot-water heater is gas. We can be without power for a week and the only thing we'll miss is television."

"I don't watch television."

"Then you should be fine."

He growled as if annoyed with the inconvenience of humbling himself to go to the home of an employee, and she said a silent prayer that he'd be stubborn enough—or maybe independent enough—to decide he'd rather sit alone in the office, maybe reading files by the emergency lights in the corridor, than go with her.

Please, God...

He pulled in a breath. "Okay. Fine. Let me get my coat."

CHAPTER THREE

THEY stepped out into the parking lot and Cullen motioned to the right. "That's my rental car."

"And it's a fine car," Wendy said, "but with power lines down, we can't drive. We don't want to become part of the problem."

Cullen ignored her sarcasm in favor of more pressing concerns. "Part of the problem?"

"We could get halfway home, come across a tree that's down and either have to leave our cars in the middle of the road or drive back here and walk anyway."

She faced him. Sunlight sparkled off the thick ice on the trees surrounding the parking lot, encircling her with a glow that made her look like a shimmering angel. He shook his head to clear the haze, but there was no haze. She truly sparkled in the icy world they were caught in.

"So what do you say we skip the first few steps we know might not work, and just walk?"

Great. Maybe a little exercise would help him get himself back to normal around her. "Fine."

"Good. You can carry Harry."

He gaped at her. "Carry Harry?"

"It's a ten-minute walk. And he's a forty-pound kid. Are

you telling me that rich guys are too soft to carry forty-pound kids?"

He snatched the little boy off the ground and hoisted him to his shoulder. Not that he took her bait about him being soft. He liked Harry. Who wouldn't? The kid had suffered the kind of loss that would flatten most adults, yet he was taking it like a man. He deserved a little special treatment.

"You have a smart mouth."

She grimaced. "Not usually."

He didn't want to hear that. He didn't want to know that she was behaving out of character in his presence. It was confirmation that she was attracted to him, too. If they were attracted to each other and about to spend the night together that might be trouble. Of course, if she was being smart with him it could be because she didn't like the attraction any more than he did—which should make them perfectly safe.

Occupied with his thoughts, Cullen slipped on the ice and bobbled Harry, who squealed with delight. "This is fun!"

"Always happy to oblige," Cullen told Harry, before he leaned toward Wendy and whispered, "Italian loafers weren't made for walking on ice."

"It's a very short walk. Ten minutes tops." She pointed to the grassy strip beside the sidewalk. "But if I were you I'd walk in that."

He stepped into the bumpier grass and found the footing a little more solid. Harry groaned. "Darn."

With his hands on Harry's thighs, holding him on his shoulders, Cullen shook his head. "Kids. You think the weirdest things are fun."

Harry giggled. Cullen's spirits unexpectedly lifted, but he told himself to settle down. He might want to make Harry's life a little brighter, but he wasn't here for fun and games. He had to work with Wendy Winston for the next few weeks. He had to be nice to her, but he also had to keep his distance. He didn't want to accidentally start a relationship that would have to end when he left.

He stayed quiet the rest of the way to her home. Walking on the grass, he managed to slip only a time or two, but that provided Harry with a few laughs, and Wendy with something to talk about with Harry.

Suddenly she turned up an icy walkway to the right, and Cullen stopped.

Oh. Dear. God.

"Come on."

Swallowing back a protest, Cullen carefully navigated the walkway and the five icy stairs to the wide front porch. They stepped inside a freezing-cold foyer with beautiful hardwood floors, a new paint job and a modern table holding a ginger-jar lamp and a stack of unopened mail.

She stripped off her coat. "As soon as I light the fireplace and turn on the oven, the downstairs will be toasty warm." Heading for the kitchen, she called over her shoulder, "If you're cold, don't take off your coat until the place heats up."

He slid Harry to the floor. The little boy immediately shucked his coat, found the hall closet and tossed it inside. Cullen grimaced. He'd look like a real wimp if he stayed in his coat, so he shrugged it off and followed Harry into the kitchen.

Wendy beamed at Harry. "Oh, you took off your own coat!"

Harry nodded. "I saw you put it in the closet before so I know what to do now."

Cullen caught the exchange but he was too busy staring at the kitchen cabinets to comment.

Wendy winced. "I know they're ugly."

"My father hated them, too."

Her pretty green eyes widened. "This was your house? Your family was the rich family that left town and neglected it?"

"That would be us."

"And your mother is responsible for this floor?"

He shrugged. "It was the eighties. Linoleum was all the rage."

"Yeah, but now I'm stuck with it. I should shoot at least one of you."

Cullen heard her, but didn't respond. Memories of conversations over breakfast with Gabby, the Barrington's housekeeper, came tumbling back.

Are you ever going to learn to make pancakes?

No.

I like pancakes!

Little boys aren't supposed to get everything they want. Makes them spoiled.

Gabby hadn't been mean about it. She'd laughed. She was a fun, easygoing woman who sometimes even sat at the table and ate scrambled eggs and toast with him before she drove him to school.

"I asked if you wanted anything to drink."

Hearing Wendy's question, he spun to face her. Standing by the open refrigerator, she held a pitcher of something pink. "What is it?"

"Pink lemonade."

"Got any bottled water?"

"I have tap water."

"That's fine."

"Glasses are in the cupboard." She pointed at the one by the sink. "Help yourself."

Walking to the sink, he watched her pour a drink for Harry and one for herself then carry eggs, butter and milk to the center island after storing the lemonade. He tried to remember his mom even being in the kitchen, let alone cooking, and not one memory surfaced.

"We're baking cookies, if you want to help."

He turned at Wendy's question. Her smile was forced. Her eyes not as bright as they had been. She obviously didn't want his help and he wasn't really in the mood to remember things that only made him a weird combination of angry and sad.

"No, if you have a book somewhere I wouldn't mind passing the time reading."

She relaxed. "I have a roomful of bookcases stuffed with just about anything you could want. Third door…"

"On the right. I know. It used to be a library and office. That's why there are built-in bookcases."

"Okay. Just open the drapes. When it starts to get dark, we'll break out the candles and flashlights."

"Great."

He entered the library feeling a mix of nostalgia and disappointment. His mother had worked in this room every night and most weekends. But Wendy didn't have a desk and leather chairs. Instead, a chaise sat by the bay window. A well-worn yellow comforter lay across the foot. The room that had been a place of work was now a place of peace and quiet. He scanned her titles, found a thriller by a favorite author, and settled in on the chaise.

After an hour, the scent of fresh-baked cookies drifted into the room. He closed the book and inhaled deeply before rising from the chaise and walking into the kitchen.

"Smells good in here."

Green icing on the tip of his nose and flour across one cheek, Harry grinned at him from his chair beside the kitchen island. "I'm painting stained-glass windows on a church."

Cullen laughed. "No kidding!"

Wendy looked offended. "Hey, I can get pretty fancy with my cookies."

Glancing at the rows of already painted cookies on the far end of the island, Cullen nodded. "So I see."

Harry nodded. "You paint one, Mr...."

"This is Mr. Barrington," Wendy supplied.

"Since we're kind of in close quarters and unusual circumstances I think you might as well call me Cullen."

"Okay, Cullen!" Harry said, handing him a cookie. "You paint this one. It's a bell."

"I see that."

"So paint it."

"With frosting," Wendy qualified. "But you should also wash your hands first."

He was going to say no. He'd never done anything like this in his life and he was too old to start now. But just the mention of the word *frosting* squeezed his heart. Unable to catch every word said about him, Harry had repeated what he thought he'd heard and had called himself a frosting child. In a way he was. He was a sweet little boy left in the hands of a cold, sterile system. How could Cullen turn away the request of a child who'd just lost his mother?

"Okay."

He washed his hands, picked up his cookie again and chose a paintbrush from those assembled beside the colorful cups of frosting. He watched Wendy dip her brush into the yellow icing and paint the bell she held a bright yellow, then switch brushes to add red icing to create a bow. He mimicked her movements, except he dipped his brush in blue. He covered his cookie in pale-blue frosting and painted the bow shape at the top white.

Harry approved it with a smile. "I like it."

"I like it, too, but you know what? I'm kind of getting hungry."

Wendy said, "Let me finish up here and I'll make hamburgers."

"Actually, I make a great hamburger. You said your gas stove will work, right?"

She nodded. "That's how we made these cookies."

"Then you guys just go ahead and keep painting. I'll make burgers and by the time you're done, dinner will be ready."

Wendy smiled. Cullen's heart tripped over itself in his chest. Now that they were in a comfortable environment, he'd begun thinking of things a little more normally. But that wasn't necessarily good. Instead of envisioning off-the-wall images like sparkling angels when he looked at her, he was now thinking how he'd like to kiss the lips that had pulled upward into a smile. They were a soft reddish color. Untarnished by lipstick or gloss. Very real. Plump. Tempting.

But that was wrong. They'd be working together for the next weeks. Visions of angels were one thing. Actually wanting to kiss his employee was another. Anything he said or did could turn into a sexual-harassment suit. He had to stop this and stop it right now.

He walked to the refrigerator and pulled out the hamburger. "What's going to happen to everything in your refrigerator if the power stays out for a long time?"

"If we don't open the refrigerator often, lots of it will be okay. Plus, I have blocks of ice in the freezer for times when this happens. It acts like a big cooler. Everything in there will stay frozen and I can put the important things from the refrigerator in there, if I need to."

"You're pretty smart."

Holding a cookie she'd just painted with bright-red frosting, she laughed. "Yeah. Right."

Happy to have their minds back on work, he said, "You are. All your performance appraisals say that."

"You read my performance appraisals?"

"I read your file this morning. You are my administrative assistant for the next four weeks. I figured I'd better know who I was getting."

"Oh." She placed her cookie on the aluminum foil that lined the far end of the island and reached for another one. "So, how did you learn to cook?"

He grimaced. "Our housekeeper taught me."

"That's right. Your mom was the last company president."

He nodded. "My dad owned an investment firm and my mom ran the factory, so my parents were overly busy. Our housekeeper was the one who fed me, nudged me to get dressed, drove me to school…" He pointed at the stove. "And taught me to cook. Nothing fancy, just the basics. Eggs. Hamburgers." He shrugged. "That kind of stuff."

"So that makes you pretty handy to have around the house."

He laughed. "And also a good roommate for everybody in college."

"Where did you go to school?"

He could tell she was only making casual conversation, but he nonetheless felt odd, as if he were bragging and he winced. "Harvard."

"Ah. Right."

"Where'd you go to school?"

"Community college for two years, then I met my husband and realized I could be an administrative assistant while he did his internship at the local hospital. When he died, I probably should have gone back for a degree." She shrugged. "But I just never found anything I wanted to study."

"I'm sorry. I didn't mean to pry."

* * *

With her focus on choosing the next cookie to paint, Wendy shrugged again. "It's all right." She said the well-practiced words easily, but the emptiness that shuddered through her contradicted them. Still, as she'd told Harry, she shouldn't dwell. She'd moved on. Gotten tougher, smarter. "It's been two years since Greg died."

Surveying the cookies to be painted, Harry casually said, "Cullen's mom died this year."

Wendy spun to face the stove. "Now, *I'm* sorry."

"As you said, it's all right. She actually died in January. So my dad and I are pretty much beyond it."

Finished patting the hamburgers into shape, Cullen poked through cupboards, looking for a frying pan. Wendy watched him, feeling a shift in the funny catch she got in her heart every time she looked at him. Hearing about his mom's death reminded her that he was as human as everybody else. But was it really good to begin seeing him as a normal man? Wasn't it wiser to continue thinking of him as a super-good-looking but unapproachable playboy?

By the time the hamburgers were ready, Wendy and Harry had finished painting their cookies, and laid them on the island to dry. Wendy pulled paper plates from the pantry and handed them to Harry.

"Since we're not sure when we'll get power again, it's probably a good idea for us not to dirty too many dishes."

Harry scurried to the round table in the corner of the room and arranged the plates in front of three chairs. Cullen set a platter of hamburgers in the center.

Wendy found the plastic cutlery and carried it to the table along with a bag of hamburger buns and a bag of potato chips. "We can eat reject cookies for dessert."

"Sounds good to me," Cullen said, pulling a seat up to the table.

But Harry stopped him. "I want to sit there!" he said, shifting Cullen to the left, to the place beside Wendy.

Wendy looked over at the little boy. He didn't seem upset. He seemed to genuinely want the seat on the end. So she said nothing. They passed the hamburgers and buns around the table, then the chips. Pale light filtered in from the windows in the top half of the back door. The sun was setting.

"I think I might need to get a candle."

"Do you want some help?"

"No, I'm fine. I just have a feeling it'll be dark before we're done eating." She rose from the table and found the big round candles and matches she kept for times the electricity failed. She lit one of the fat beige candles, set it between the hamburgers and the chips and took her seat again.

As they ate, the light from the window faded and the candle's light replaced it, creating an unfortunately romantic glow. Wendy stole a look at Cullen. He was stealing a glance at her. A sizzle of electricity arced between them. Time stood still as they simply stared into each other's eyes.

"My head looks like a watermelon," Harry said with a giggle, pointing at a shadow cast by the flickering candlelight.

Wendy laughed. It was exactly the comic relief they needed. "So does mine."

Cullen turned to see the wall behind him. He laughed. "So does mine."

Harry settled into his seat again. "I like this."

One of Cullen's black eyebrows rose. "Eating in the dark?"

"No. Laughing."

Wendy glanced at Cullen, again just as he looked at her. This time, instead of chemistry sparking between them, understanding did. This little boy had spent the past months of his life not doing anything, not going anywhere, probably never laughing.

Cullen rose and unexpectedly grabbed Harry, hoisting him over his shoulder and tickling the strip of belly exposed when his T-shirt rose. "Yeah, well, if you like to laugh so much how about this?" He tickled him again and Harry giggled with delight.

Wendy's heart melted in her chest. Never in a million years would she guess somebody like Cullen could be so perceptive, but he was and she was grateful.

"I have a good idea," she said, rising from the table. "Why don't we throw away these dishes and take the cookies into the living room? The fireplace is already lit. We'll put our sleeping bags down on the floor and make popcorn."

Cullen swung Harry to the floor. "Or we could tell ghost stories."

As Harry's small feet touched down he said, "Ghost stories?"

Cullen smiled evilly. "Oh, I know plenty. I spent some time in Gettysburg."

Harry's nose wrinkled. "You were in prison?"

Cullen and Wendy both laughed. Wendy said, "No! Gettysburg is a famous battlefield. But rather than ghost stories," she said, giving Cullen a look, hoping he'd understand, "why don't we tell funny stories?"

Harry jumped up and down. "I love funny stories!" Then he raced out of the kitchen, toward the living room.

Obviously realizing his mistake, Cullen rubbed his hand across the back of his neck. "Sorry. I forgot his mom just died or I never would have mentioned ghosts."

"That's okay. I've slipped up a time or two myself today."

He glanced around. "Have you got any marshmallows?"

Dipping into the pantry and then out again, she displayed

a bag of fat white marshmallows. "I always keep a bag on hand in case I ever want to make s'mores."

"We'll start toasting those over the fire and tell funny stories and he'll forget all about the ghosts."

Wendy smiled her agreement, but her smile faded when he turned away, gathered the catsup and mustard and walked to the refrigerator as if it were very normal for him to be in her kitchen. In a way she supposed it was. This had been his home. But she had the oddest feeling that he was right where he was supposed to be.

And so was she.

Blaming that feeling on the fact that they both called this house home, she shook her head, told herself to stop acting like an idiot and carried the marshmallows to the living room where Harry eagerly awaited her.

They spent the next hour roasting marshmallows and teasing Harry. Then Cullen realized he'd not only have to sleep in his uncomfortable clothes; he'd also have to wear them the next day unless he went to his car.

Wendy grabbed two flashlights from the kitchen and met him at the front door.

"Are you sure you're okay with this?"

"It's a ten-minute walk to my car, remember? I hadn't yet checked into my hotel, so I can grab my duffel bag and be back in twenty-two minutes."

As he spoke, he smiled down at her, and she suddenly knew why she kept getting these odd feelings. In the office when he was Cullen Barrington, owner of Barrington Candies, he was an unapproachable playboy. But here in this house where he was comfortable, with a little boy he couldn't resist being kind to, she was seeing a side of him she would bet few people— if any—had ever seen. And she was beginning to like him.

She quickly looked away and stepped back. She didn't want to like this guy. At least not romantically. This time next month, he'd probably be on a beach or in a casino. There was no sense forming an attachment. But more than that they came from two different worlds, saw life two different ways, probably had totally opposite beliefs about most things. Liking him was just wrong.

"See you when you get back."

He opened the door and pointed at his Italian loafers. "Wish me luck."

Wendy couldn't help it; she laughed. "Luck."

While he was gone, Wendy went to the storage room and found the two sleeping bags that she and her husband had used on camping trips. Because there were only two, she grabbed blankets from the linen closet and brought them along, too.

After she and Harry laid the open sleeping bags on the floor to serve as a cushion, they covered them in blankets. She took Harry upstairs, helped him wash up and eased him into his pajamas. On the way back to the living room they stopped in the library and found a tattered copy of *A Christmas Story*.

By the time Cullen returned, she'd begun reading it aloud to Harry. Cullen took his duffel bag upstairs and returned dressed in sweatpants and a T-shirt. Not interrupting her reading, he slid under the blanket on the other side of Harry. She read a few chapters until Harry's eyelids began to droop and eventually closed completely.

Wendy slid the blanket up to his chin. He snuggled into the pillow.

She glanced over at Cullen and whispered, "This wasn't exactly how I'd hoped our first night would turn out."

"This was your first day with him?"

She nodded.

He laughed softly. "I don't think Harry minded." He pulled

in a breath. "And I have to thank you, too. I'd have been sleeping on your boss's lumpy couch tonight if you hadn't come to my rescue."

"It's nothing."

"No, another employee might have been too intimidated to invite me. I appreciate that you not only opened your home, but you didn't make a big deal of it."

Cullen rose from the makeshift bed and tossed another log on the fire. Levering his hand on the coffee table, he lowered himself to the floor again, but as he pulled his hand away he jarred the table enough that the silver bell decoration in a Christmas flower arrangement rang.

Hearing the bell, Harry squeezed his eyes shut even more tightly.

Please, let Miss Wendy and Cullen get married and adopt me.

He made the wish quickly, just as he had the other two times he'd wished.

The first time he'd wished they'd get married and adopt him had been at the door of Miss Wendy's work, when she'd slipped on the ice. He'd seen her and Cullen look at each other funny like Jimmy Franklin's mom and dad looked at each other, and he knew they could be a mom and dad. *His* mom and dad. So he'd wished and when he was done wishing the bell rang.

Then, when she came back from getting the radio, she and Cullen had looked at each other funny again, he'd wished again and church bells had rung.

He snuggled more deeply into the pillow, a plan forming in his head. What if he made the wish every time he heard a bell ring? He'd tried to wish that his mom would get well and that wish hadn't worked. But maybe that was because he didn't have a bell? So this time, he'd wish every time he heard a bell. And maybe his wish would come true.

CHAPTER FOUR

WENDY woke first. Sunlight poured in from the big window behind the sofa. Guessing it was probably around nine o'clock, she sat up and her back protested.

"Floor's not the most comfortable place to sleep," Cullen whispered.

"You can say that again." She pulled in a breath and smiled ruefully. "My coffeemaker's electric, but if you'd like some tea, we can make that."

"Anything with caffeine is fine."

She rolled over to lift herself off the floor. On the other side of Harry, Cullen did the same.

While Cullen went upstairs to change out of his sweatpants and T-shirt, Wendy boiled water for tea. He returned to her kitchen dressed in dark trousers and a black-and-beige-striped sweater. Her stomach took a tumble. He was so damned good-looking.

She turned back to the stove, poured boiling water over tea bags in two cups and brought them to the table.

"You were very good with Harry last night," he said.

"You're no slouch yourself."

He laughed. "Thank you." He toyed with his tea bag. "So what's the story with him?"

"Right after he and his mom moved in next door, his mom was diagnosed with cancer." She dipped her tea bag in and pulled it out, testing the strength of her tea. "I started visiting once a week to see if she needed anything and soon I was helping her get through chemo. Eventually I was doing pretty much everything at her house." She smiled at the memory. "Including reading Harry a story every night and tucking him in."

"So social services considered you a good candidate to take him in while they look for his dad?"

She snorted a laugh. "Not even close. His mom gave me custody in her will."

"Oh."

Cullen's voice was full of such happy surprise that Wendy shook her head. "Don't get excited. His biological father has first right to custody no matter what Betsy's will says."

"But I can tell you'd really like to be the one to raise him."

She nodded. "I think I could be a great mom. I already love Harry and the thing he needs more than anything right now is just plain love."

"I'm surprised you don't have children of your own."

She licked her lips, so tempted to be honest and confide in him. But she knew the bond they'd formed over the past twenty-four hours was an aberration, so she'd tell him the basics and keep the heartache to herself. "My husband and I were waiting to be more financially secure to have children."

He inclined his head in acknowledgment, holding her gaze as if he knew there was more and waited for her to admit it. When she stayed silent, he said, "So the bottom line is your arrangement with Harry is only temporary."

The fact that he didn't probe or push relieved her as much as disappointed her. She supposed she secretly hoped he wanted the bond, but not pushing her to elaborate proved he didn't.

"There are lots of ways this could play out. They could find his dad and his dad could take him. Or they could find his dad and he could tell them he doesn't want Harry—"

Cullen's eyes widened. "Doesn't want Harry?"

She shook her head. "Harry told me he hasn't seen his dad in so long he doesn't remember what he looks like. He thinks he's in prison."

"That's not good."

Avoiding his gaze, she bobbed her tea bag in and out of the hot water in her cup. "In any event, I have him until they find his dad."

He caught her gaze. His dark eyes were serious and sincere. "That's too bad. I think you're a good pair."

She smiled. "Thanks."

The kitchen became silent as Wendy pulled her tea bag from her cup and added milk and sugar. After taking a sip, she said, "What about you?"

"What about me?"

She shrugged. "I might not have spilled the entire story of my life, but you now know things lots of people at the plant don't know. I think it's only fair you tell me something about yourself so we can keep each other's secrets."

"Honestly, there isn't much to tell. When my parents finally retired, five years ago, they moved to Miami with me, and my dad and I started a small investment firm."

"You have a job?"

"Of course I have a job."

She shook her head. "I'm sorry. I just pictured you in Miami boating, going to parties, taking private jets to Vegas to gamble."

He laughed. "I can still do all that. Rather than create a big firm like my dad had here in Pennsylvania, we kept our Miami firm small. I make appointments when I want them. Schedule myself off a lot. So your guess isn't too far off the mark."

She said, "Ah," and their gazes caught. The sizzle from the day before returned. But this time they both knew it was pointless. He was a strong man who clearly arranged his life the way he wanted it. Just as her late husband had done. Because Greg was so determined, so forceful, so focused, so sure of what he wanted, she'd lost the opportunity to have what *she* wanted…children with him. She vowed she'd never get involved with that kind of man again.

Plus, she might be bolder now, but she was still a small-town woman whose fondest wish was to get custody of the little boy next door. Even if she wanted to take a risk with her new-found independence with someone as clear about his life goals as Cullen seemed to be, she was too simple, too average to fit into his extravagant, exciting world.

They couldn't be further apart if they tried.

The refrigerator motor started. The microwave beeped. The kitchen lights popped on.

Wendy pulled away from Cullen's gaze. "Talk about timing."

He laughed and glanced down at his half-empty tea cup. "Yeah."

"So, are you ready for coffee?"

He shook his head. "I'll get some on the way to the office."

"Do you want me to come in?"

"I'll be fine." He rose from the table. "If Harry's awake I'll say goodbye."

She nodded. Cullen turned and walked out of the kitchen.

Wendy put a pot of coffee together and dropped four slices of bread into the toaster.

A few minutes later, Cullen returned to the kitchen, carrying his duffel bag. "He's still asleep."

"I'll tell him you said goodbye."

"Okay." He turned and headed for the foyer and the front door. A polite hostess, Wendy followed him.

He faced her with a smile. "Thanks for everything."

Her nerves spiked with the sense that his leaving was all wrong, even though she knew it wasn't. There was no reason for him to stay. No reason for her to ask him to stay, except that she enjoyed his company, and they'd already figured out there was no point to that.

Wendy pulled in a breath. "You're welcome."

"I'll see you tomorrow."

She nodded.

He caught her gaze. She smiled slightly. He didn't seem to want to go any more than she wanted him to. A second spun into ten; ten seconds stretched into half a minute. Finally, with their gazes clinging, he lowered his head and touched his mouth to hers.

She wasn't so much surprised by the fact that he'd kissed her as she was by the power in one brush of his lips across hers. The electric sparks they'd been throwing to each other for the past twenty-four hours all congealed and shot lightning through her.

He slowly pulled away, his eyes bright, his expression as dumbfounded as she felt.

"I'll see you at the office tomorrow."

She whispered, "Okay."

And then he was gone. He wouldn't be this warm, this open, this honest with her at the candy factory. She'd never see this Cullen Barrington again.

Wendy was glad for the distraction her curious six-year-old provided. She let him help make eggs and toast for breakfast, then bundled him in his jacket and mittens and took him to the mall.

"What are we shopping for?"

She smiled down at him. "I have three brothers and a mom, so every year I buy each of them a Christmas gift."

"Cool."

"If you're still with me at Christmas, I'll be taking you to Ohio with me for the holiday."

His blue eyes widened. "Out of town?"

She laughed. Everything was an adventure to this child. "Yes."

"Cool."

She laughed and he tugged on her hand to get her attention again.

"Do you think we could buy a bell for Creamsicle?"

"A bell for Creamsicle?"

Behind the brown-framed glasses, Harry's big blue eyes blinked at her. "Yeah."

"Why do you want him to have a bell?"

He tilted his head. "Because it's Christmas?"

"Oh, a *Christmas* bell!"

He smiled. "Yeah."

"I'm not sure he'll wear it, but he does wear a collar. So why don't we look for a new collar with a bell?"

Harry nodded eagerly. "Okay!"

They found a bright red-and-green collar for Creamsicle, complete with a small red sleigh bell. Harry tucked the little bag into the pocket of his jacket with a smile. They shopped for another hour, ate dinner at a local fast-food restaurant and returned home.

Harry immediately yanked the cat collar from his jacket pocket. "Here, Creamsicle!"

"He's not going to come," Wendy said.

Harry ignored her, running to the steps and calling upstairs. "Come here, Creamsicle!"

A few seconds later the rotund orange-and-white cat came thumping down the steps. At the bottom, he wound around Wendy's feet, then Harry's.

Wendy smiled. "He likes you."

Harry peered up at her. "I know." He crouched down and tried to work the buckle on the old collar.

Wendy stooped down beside him. "Here. Let me. I forgot how old this collar was. It was probably time to replace it anyway."

She made short order of the old collar and helped Harry slide the new one around Creamsicle's neck. The cat nudged them both as if saying thanks, and walked away.

Harry frowned. "It doesn't ring."

"It's a small bell. So Creamsicle will have to do something like jump for it to ring."

The little boy considered that then grinned. "That will make it special when it rings, right?"

"Exactly."

Harry's grin grew. Wendy shook her head and led him into the kitchen for a snack. She'd never seen a kid who got such pleasure from little things the way Harry did.

Tired from the day out, Harry fell asleep on the sofa and Wendy carried him up to bed.

When she returned downstairs, she tuned the television to one of her favorite shows, but without the distraction of Harry, her mind drifted back to that kiss with Cullen.

She pressed her fingers to her lips. It was hard to believe that a man like Cullen would find her attractive, let alone that he'd kiss her. But she did eventually make some sense of it.

In their discussion over tea, they'd realized how different they were. They both knew nothing would come of this attraction, so maybe he felt safe in kissing her? He probably considered it a one-time thing. A chance to give in to the attraction, albeit a little, just for a taste.

The very notion made her dreamy and she sighed heavily. Was it so wrong to want a little romance in her life? Just a little. Just something to make her believe that someday she would find somebody else.

Realizing the television show wasn't going to hold her attention, she walked back down the hall to the library, found a book and went to bed.

Because she read most of the night, she woke late and the morning routine she'd envisioned with Harry went to hell. The twenty minutes they had before Harry had to be at school were pure chaos. She'd called the principal on Friday morning, after she'd gotten word that she would get Harry on Saturday morning, and had had them reactivate his records. He was actually returning to the very class he'd left. That part of things worked out so well that she couldn't let him be late for his first day back. She quickly dressed Harry and herself and headed out the door to drive him to school.

She took him to the office where one of the administrative assistants walked him to the room he already knew. Happy that she'd gotten him to school on time, she breathed a sigh of relief, then realized getting him to school on time had made *her* late. She thanked the principal and raced out of the building to her car.

Even driving as fast as was allowed on the quiet streets of Barrington, she was twenty minutes late for work.

At her desk she shucked her coat and scarf, waving silent

hellos to coworkers who said good morning as they passed her door, and walked to the open door of Cullen's office.

Dressed in a dark suit with white shirt and pale-blue tie, he looked as good—as yummy—as he always did.

"Sorry I'm late."

He glanced up from the computer. Their eyes met. Everything female in her burst with life and energy just from the look in his beautiful dark eyes. It was all she could do not to sigh with longing.

Instead, she cleared her throat. "Harry and I had trouble getting accustomed to our morning routine." There was no way she'd tell him that she'd overslept because she hadn't been able to sleep the night before because she'd been thinking about how he'd kissed her. He might be attracted to her, but he'd made his choice. And she'd made hers. Attracted or not, they weren't a good match.

"Ah. First day of school."

"I was lucky enough to get him back into the class he was in before his mom died."

"That's great." He glanced down at his desk then up at her again. "Did you tell him I had to leave? That's why I didn't say goodbye?"

She nodded. "He wants me to invite you to dinner."

He laughed. "Tell him thanks." He paused then added, "But just between you and me, I don't think that's a good idea."

Staring into his dark eyes, she wanted to sigh with disappointment, but they'd actually come to this conclusion at the breakfast table Sunday morning. They were attracted, but different. Too different really to have a relationship. No matter how good the kiss at her door.

"Okay." She took a careful step into the room. "Is there anything you need me to do this morning?"

"I'm fine for now." He caught her gaze again. "But I'd like you to walk with me into the plant when I make my morning rounds."

"To introduce you?"

He nodded.

She smiled. "Okay. Just let me know when you're ready."

She left his office extremely proud of both of them. They were adults who knew better than to give in to silly chemistry. There were too many differences between them. They came from two different worlds. Wanted two different kinds of lives. So they were being smart. Savvy.

It was nearly lunchtime before Cullen had her guide him through the plant. He'd already met with the supervisors, so his trek around the manufacturing floor was to give the regular employees a chance to get comfortable with him.

They stepped through the door separating the office from the cooking area and were immediately immersed in the scent of chocolate. The men by the kettles grunted greetings, but otherwise kept to their work. The men watching the assembly line where chocolate poured over creamy centers, smiled and said, "Hello."

But the female candy packers visibly stared as Wendy introduced him to the group in general.

"These are the first-shift packers."

Cullen smiled and nodded. "Ladies."

"Good morning, Mr. Barrington."

"And back here we have shipping and receiving."

A titter of giggles followed them as they walked away. Wendy pressed her lips together to keep from laughing herself. Cullen had just made himself the object of everybody's fantasies and today's lunchtime topic of conversation.

After visiting the remaining departments, they returned to their work space.

Cullen paused by her desk. "They all seem like very nice people."

He said it as if that surprised him and Wendy gaped at him. "Of course they're nice!"

He rubbed his hand along the back of his neck. "Yes. Of course."

With that, he went into his office and closed the door. Wendy stared at it for a few seconds, thinking his comment was odd, but shook her head to clear it of any thought of Cullen. It was better not to get too involved, especially not to try to figure him out. Plus, it was time for her to go to lunch.

In the small lunchroom, she pulled her brown bag from the refrigerator and made her way to the table where her two friends sat.

"He's cute!" Emma Watson said before Wendy even sat down. Ten years older than Wendy, Emma was a short brunette, married with two kids.

"Yes, he is."

"And you're single," Patty Franks reminded her. A fortyish blonde, recently divorced, Patty continually tried to get Wendy to hit the bar scene with her.

Wendy laughed. "He is a rich man with an exciting life in Miami. What the heck would he want with a little Pennsylvania bumpkin like me?"

Emma and Patty exchanged a look. Emma sighed. "Uh, Miss Pennsylvania Bumpkin, it seems to me you were married to a doctor. I'm guessing you have to know you're the kind of woman a rich guy wants on his arm."

Wendy gaped at her. "You think I want to be on some guy's arm?"

Patty pressed her hand to her chest. "I would kill to be able to attract a guy like that. You should be dressing a little better," she said, pointing at Wendy's simple red sweater. "Wearing perfume. Tempting him."

Wendy's mouth fell open. "Are you nuts?"

"I saw him looking at you," Emma said slyly. "He likes you."

Wendy felt a blush creeping into her cheeks. Maybe she and Cullen weren't as good at hiding their attraction as they believed. A little honesty was the only thing that would nip this in the bud. "Even if we were attracted, think it through. We aren't suited."

"I'm almost tempted to ask you to pretend you are." Patti leaned close to Wendy and whispered, "We could use a spy. There's a rumor going around that he's actually here to close the plant."

Wendy gasped. "That's not true!"

Emma said, "How do you know?"

"Yeah," Patty seconded. "How do you know?"

"Because I know."

"You don't think it's odd that Mr. McCoy suddenly decided to go on vacation?"

"No."

"Or that *the* Cullen Barrington decided to step in for him?"

It *was* odd, and Cullen had behaved oddly on Saturday morning, not letting her see the letters he'd typed. Plus, there was the matter of the missing final copy of the forecast.

She gave herself a mental shake. The company made too much money for Cullen simply to close it. With the profits the company made, the Barringtons shouldn't even be considering selling it. But she couldn't tell her friends that. She knew how much money the company made because she typed the financial reports. Confidentiality precluded her from discussing what she saw.

"No, I don't think it's odd that Mr. Barrington is standing in for Mr. McCoy. I think he has his reasons. He could be here simply because it's been five years since his family were directly involved with the plant. They might have decided it was time one of them was."

"Maybe. But you can't explain away the fact that we haven't gotten a raise since his mom retired. No raises usually means things aren't going well. Now that the Barringtons are in Miami, they don't care about us. They could close this factory—" she snapped her fingers "—like that."

"No. Stop!" Wendy held up her hand. Patty was interpreting the facts all wrong, but Wendy couldn't talk about what she knew from typing confidential financial statements. With everything going on in her life, she also didn't have the quickness of mind to make up an alternative story. "I don't have the brain power to think about this right now. Even if I would date him to spy for you guys, I can't. My plate is full with Harry—"

Patty put her elbow on the table and her chin on her fist. "Really? There's a good chance they'll find his dad tomorrow and Harry won't be an issue."

Only Emma or Patty could be this brutally honest with her, and though right at this minute she wished they couldn't, she also saw Patty's point.

"I just don't want to see you lose a good opportunity," Patty said. "Guys like Cullen Barrington only come along once in a lifetime. If you're not following up on your attraction because of Harry, you could be making a big mistake."

She shook her head. "There's no point to following up when we don't want the same things."

"How do you know you don't want the same things?"

Wendy glanced over at Patty. Damn the woman was quick. But Wendy was quicker.

"Did you look at him? His clothes scream designer names. My clothes are from a discount department store. I don't fit into his world. That is, if he'd even want to make room in his world."

Emma sighed. "You're a pessimist."

Wendy took a bite of her sandwich, chewed and swallowed then said, "I'm a realist." She glanced around to make sure no one else was paying attention then she added, "You guys know what happened with Greg. I let him make all the decisions because he was so sure of where he wanted to go and it cost me the opportunity to have a child."

Emma frowned. Patty rolled her eyes. "So don't let this one make all the decisions."

Wendy toyed with her sandwich. "Not all men are like Greg, but Cul—Mr. Barrington is. Just from the way he works, I can tell he's a man accustomed to giving orders and getting his own way." She wouldn't tell them about his investment-counseling business, about being able to arrange his life any way he wanted, that would prove they'd had a private conversation. As much as she loved Emma and Patty, the gossip would spread like wildfire and Cullen's stay would be hell for both of them. "I want a man who wants a partner, not arm candy."

"Arm candy." Both Emma and Patty grinned.

Emma said, "How appropriate for a guy who owns a candy factory."

"You guys are hopeless." She pulled in a breath and changed the subject. "Things went very well with Harry this weekend."

Emma grinned. "So how does it feel to be a mom?"

"I wouldn't know. I'm not letting myself feel too much. Just as you said, they could find Harry's dad tomorrow."

The buzzer sounded, signaling the end of the lunch break, and Wendy made her way back to her desk and resumed her typical Monday chores. Around two o'clock, Cullen stepped out of his office and handed her some notes he wanted typed. When he returned to his office, he left the door open.

Wendy immediately went to work on the notes. She typed them quickly, e-mailed them to his computer, printed them and slid the hard copy onto his desk.

Without looking up, Cullen said, "Thanks."

Happy that they were behaving like a typical boss and assistant, she returned to her desk and went back to work.

On Tuesday everybody still gossiped about why *the* Cullen Barrington would stand in for the plant manager. Finishing up the Christmas rush might be the reason. But that only spurred more questions that rumbled through the workers on the plant floor. Why had Mr. McCoy taken a vacation during their busiest time of the year? Had he been fired? Was the plant about to close?

Wednesday at lunch, Patty and Emma speculated that Cullen had asked Mr. McCoy to take a vacation and was there as a spy of some sort. That made Wendy laugh. "I can understand you wanting to spy on him. But why would he spy on us? What could he possibly be looking for?"

That stopped Patty cold and made Emma frown in consternation.

At lunch on Thursday they decided he was looking for ways to make his father and himself more money from the factory, and that, Wendy had to concede, made at least a bit of sense.

It actually calmed the gossip, until Emma said, "And if he doesn't, we're history." Then that rumor caught fire and spread throughout the factory.

On Friday the conversation mercifully turned to everybody's plans for the weekend. Patty had a date. Emma was taking her kids for pictures on Santa's lap. Wendy's heart stuttered with joy at just the thought of getting Harry's picture taken on Santa's lap. Also, involving Harry with other kids, especially for a holiday reason, was a good idea.

"Can Harry and I meet you at the mall at about one o'clock?"

Patty rose from the lunch table. "Sounds great. I can't wait to meet him."

"You'll love him."

Wendy made her way back to the office amazed that within six short days she'd not only gotten the hang of thinking of Harry first, but also that the rumors of the plant closing seemed to have died down, if only for the weekend.

At about a quarter to three she heard a noise, looked up and saw Randy Zamias walking into her office.

She pulled in a breath. "Mr. Zamias."

Tall and thin, wearing a neat-as-a-pin brown-tweed suit, Harry's case worker took the remaining steps to her desk. "Ms. Winston."

Because she didn't have a seat in her office to offer him, she rose. "How can I help you?"

"I'm afraid I have some unfortunate news."

"News?"

"Yes, we've located Harry's father."

Her heart stopped. She told herself that Harry would be better off with his biological father, but Harry didn't remember his father. Fear coursed through her. "You have?"

Randy cleared his throat. "Unfortunately, he's dead."

This time the world spun. "That's..." She swallowed, as mixed feelings danced around inside her. Even as her heart swelled at the prospect of getting Harry, it also broke for the little boy who now had no parents. "That's sad for Harry."

Randy pushed his glasses up his long, thin nose. He pulled in a breath. "He was killed in a fight in the prison yard three years ago."

Right about when Harry said he'd last seen his dad. Wendy fell to her seat. "Oh, my God."

Randy sighed heavily. "Betsy had been informed, but by that time she'd divorced him." He shook his head. "There's a lot Betsy didn't tell us when we visited her."

Wendy could only stare at him. The knowledge that Harry's dad was dead was difficult, but she understood Betsy's reasons for not being forthcoming with Mr. Zamias. She had been ill and protecting her child.

Cullen stepped out of his office. He looked from Randy to Wendy and back to Randy again. His eyes narrowed. "Can I help you?"

Wendy quickly said, "This is Mr. Zamias. He's Harry's case worker from social services." She motioned toward Cullen. "And this is Cullen Barrington."

Randy's entire demeanor changed. He went from being a stiff and formal prude, to being awestruck in the blink of an eye. He stuck out his hand to shake Cullen's. "Mr. Barrington! Such a pleasure to have you back in town."

"I'm only here for a few weeks." Cullen turned to Wendy. "Are you okay?"

"Mr. Zamias just told me that Harry's dad is dead."

Cullen looked shocked. "Oh. I'm sorry."

Randy frowned. His beady brown eyes narrowed. His voice dripped with disdain when he said, "So it appears custody falls to you, Ms. Winston."

Not knowing what to say, Wendy stayed silent. She knew Randy Zamias wasn't thrilled with the way she'd demanded the rights granted to her by Betsy's will while social services searched for Harry's father. But with the news of Harry's dad's death, she became Harry's guardian. End of story.

"Don't get smug," Randy said, folding his arms on his

chest. "The will may give you custody, but because Harry was in our system, we can check up on him. Check up on *you*."

Wendy suspected Randy was only blustering because she'd challenged him, but before she could say something concil-iatory to smooth things over, Cullen walked to Randy and slid his arm across his shoulders. "If it makes you feel any better, I've been interacting with Harry since he's been in Ms. Winston's custody."

"You have?"

"Yes. If you're concerned about this transition period, I'm in Barrington until Christmas. I can continue to help out while Harry gets adjusted."

"That does make me feel better."

"Great," Cullen said, leading Randy to the door.

Watching the exchange, Wendy didn't know whether to be grateful or appalled. Cullen had taken the entire discussion out of her hands. He hadn't even given her a chance to be her own diplomat. If she had any doubts that Cullen was exactly like Greg, he'd just eliminated them.

The second Randy was out of hearing range, Cullen spun to face her. "What the heck did you do to get on his bad side?"

"When Betsy died, Harry was put into foster care because I didn't know about the will. None of us did." She pulled in a breath and caught Cullen's gaze. "When her lawyer finally contacted me, I immediately petitioned the courts to get Harry while they searched for his dad."

"You made him look bad to his superiors."

"I wasn't saying he made a bad decision, just an ill-informed one. None of us knew about Betsy's will. It wasn't anyone's fault that Harry had gone into a foster home. But I didn't want Harry to be with people he didn't know when he could have been with me." She paused. Though it felt odd to thank him for high-handing her, she knew she had to. "I guess I should thank you for smoothing things over."

"Save your thanks. I might just become a thorn in your side. Since I told old Randy I'd help with the transition, I'll have to take Harry up on his offer of dinner every few nights."

"That I can handle." Sort of. She wasn't happy he had insinuated himself into her life, but she did know his offer had given Randy a graceful out in their situation and he probably wouldn't bother them. Harry was all hers to raise—

She stopped her thoughts as a terrible realization occurred to her. With Harry now officially in her custody, everything to do with the little boy was her responsibility.

She looked at Cullen again. "I have to tell Harry that his father is dead."

CHAPTER FIVE

"Do you want me to be there?"

Wendy bit her lip, considering that. Cullen had promised Randy Zamias he would be part of things while he was in town, but she didn't want Harry to see Cullen in such an important role that he'd grow to depend on him and have a hole in his life when Cullen returned to Miami.

Still, this was a delicate situation and the more people Harry had around him for support, the better.

She glanced at her watch. "I've hired a babysitter who's been staying with him after school until I return from work. I'm trying to decide if it's better to let him have another afternoon of thinking he's got at least some family, or if I should just go home and be honest."

"Let's go be honest."

Leave it to Cullen to make the decision for her. In another twenty seconds she would have said the same thing. Yet, he beat her to the punch. Still, in this case, it really didn't matter. Harry would appreciate having Cullen around when he got the news about his dad. Anything else was irrelevant.

"Okay. Let's go."

They drove their separate cars to her house. Wendy parked

in the driveway beside the babysitter's SUV. Cullen parked on the tree-lined street in front of her house. The ice from the storm over the weekend had melted. Broken limbs had been cleared away. The sun smiled down from a bright-blue sky, but the air was cold, promising that before too long there would be snow on the ground, a sparkling white blanket for Christmas.

She walked into her warm kitchen, where Mrs. Brennon was setting a mug of steaming hot cocoa beside a plate of iced Christmas cookies for Harry's after-school snack.

"Mrs. Winston!"

"Hi, Mrs. Brennon. I know I'm early today but I really need to talk with Harry."

Cullen walked in the kitchen door behind her.

Harry's face instantly brightened. "Cullen!" He bounced off the chair and raced to Cullen to hug him around the thighs. "I missed you."

Cullen stooped down. "Hey, kid."

Harry glanced at Cullen's topcoat, black suit and silk tie. "Were you at work?"

Cullen nodded. "Yeah. With Wendy."

Wendy tapped Harry's shoulder to get his attention. "Why don't you and Cullen eat those cookies while I spend a minute with Mrs. Brennon?"

"Sure!" Taking Cullen's hand, Harry led him to the table.

Wendy directed Mrs. Brennon to the front foyer. She explained that they'd gotten the news that Harry's dad had passed away and they needed to tell him.

Mrs. Brennon's eyes filled with tears. "How sad for that sweet little boy."

"I know."

The babysitter walked to the closet and pulled out her winter coat, mittens and scarf. "I'll just be on my way then."

"Thanks. We'll see you on Monday."

Mrs. Brennon said goodbye and exited through the front door.

Wendy took a deep breath then walked into the kitchen. Cullen had removed his topcoat and hung it on a hook beside the door. He sat at the table eating cookies with Harry.

"Hey, guys."

"Hey, Wendy." Harry peered at her above his glasses. "Cullen likes my cookies better than yours."

"Well, yours were definitely prettier." She took another breath. "How about if we go into the living room for a minute to talk about something?"

Harry grabbed two cookies. "Sure."

He scrambled into the living room ahead of them. Without speaking, Cullen and Wendy followed him. He bounced onto the sofa. Wendy sat on one side. Cullen sat on the other.

"Randy Zamias from social services came to see me today." Harry wrinkled his nose. "He's bad."

"No. He's trying to look out for your welfare," Wendy said. "But he also had some news."

When Harry didn't answer, Cullen touched his forearm and Harry faced him. "About your dad."

Harry looked at Wendy. "My dad?"

"Yes, honey. Randy was searching for your dad and he found him. But he's... Well, he's..."

"He's like my mom, isn't he?"

Wendy nodded. "Yes. I'm sorry. He died."

It took a few seconds for that to really sink in, and when it did, Harry's little face crumpled and tears welled in his eyes.

Wendy took his free hand, as Cullen grabbed the cookies that were falling from his other hand. Harry hadn't seen his father since he was three. Technically, he'd lost his dad years ago. Wendy knew his tears weren't so much from loss, but from fear. Now he was totally alone.

"But this really doesn't change anything. You and I are together. I'm your mom now."

His head down, Harry said, "But it's just us." Tears dropped to his blue-jean-covered thighs. In the silence, Wendy could hear fat Creamsicle thump down the stairs and amble into the room.

Over Harry's bowed head, Wendy met Cullen's gaze. She didn't have a clue how to respond. She knew exactly what Harry meant. He had lost everyone in his life. With only her as a guardian, how could she promise him that he wouldn't someday find himself alone again?

Cullen gave her a look that nudged her to be honest. To say what she felt.

"No matter what happens, I'll be here for you, Harry. I love you."

Creamsicle picked that exact second to jump up on the sofa and into Harry's lap. He nuzzled his nose against Harry's chin. As he did, the little red bell on his collar finally rang.

Harry's head jerked up. He looked from Cullen to Wendy and back at Creamsicle again. Then he rubbed his face in the thick fur of the cat's neck. "Thanks, Creamsicle."

Wendy's heart splintered. She'd never known her ornery cat to be affectionate with anybody but her, but right at that moment she was abundantly glad he'd taken to Harry.

"Okay," Cullen said, rising from the sofa. "Since this has been a bad day, I'm going to take you both out to dinner."

Harry sighed. "I don't want to go anywhere."

"Then," Wendy said, deliberately brightening her voice, not really angry with Cullen for trying to cheer Harry, but noticing again that he never asked. He simply told. "Why don't we make something fun for supper? Like spaghetti?"

Harry's sullen expression didn't change.

Cullen said, "Or hot dogs? We could roast hot dogs here in the fireplace. My dad and I used to do it all the time."

That perked Harry up. "You did?"

"Sure."

"And then we'll make s'mores," Wendy added, leading the men into the kitchen.

They managed to keep Harry entertained all evening, tiring him out so much that when he finally took a bath and went to bed, he fell asleep immediately.

As they closed the door on his bedroom, Wendy began to feel guilty for judging Cullen so harshly. His behavior that evening had proven he truly liked Harry, and only wanted what was best for the little boy in her care. She should appreciate the fact that Cullen had smoothed things over with Randy and invited them to dinner. After all, it wasn't as if he were high-handing her into a relationship. He was being kind to her little boy.

Walking down the stairs, Wendy said, "Thanks for your help."

"You could have handled it."

That made her feel a little bit better. "Yeah, but your expertise about roasting hot dogs in the fireplace definitely came in handy."

Thinking he would be leaving, Wendy walked to the front door, but Cullen passed her and returned to the living room. He grabbed the paper plates and chocolate-bar wrappers from the s'mores. As he straightened from the coffee table, he turned to the fireplace mantel and he stopped.

Setting the candy-bar wrappers on the paper plate, he walked over to the mantel, and lifted the picture of Greg holding a fishing pole.

"Is this your husband?"

"Yes."

"He was a fisherman?" he asked brightly, obviously pleased they had something in common.

Realizing he'd gotten the wrong impression, Wendy snorted a laugh. "Not at all."

"So there's a story behind this?"

"Not really. More like a boring joke. Not something you'd be interested in." She gave what she hoped was a conversation-ending reply, grabbed the napkins from the coffee table and gathered the unopened chocolate bars and graham crackers.

Now that it had sunk in that she was really Harry's mom, she had yet another reason not to get involved with Cullen. Forget about the fact that he was her boss and they weren't a good match; too much involvement between her and Cullen meant Harry could be hurt when he returned to Miami. As long as he was just a guy who came to dinner once or twice to visit Harry, Harry would be okay. But if Harry saw her and Cullen being romantic, he'd get all the wrong ideas and a little boy who'd already suffered enough hurt in one lifetime would once again be disappointed. It was best to keep things simple between her and Cullen.

In her peripheral vision, she saw him shake his head, just before he turned and walked through the foyer toward the kitchen.

Carrying the candy bars and graham crackers, she followed him. He dropped his trash into the receptacle, while she stored the extra chocolate and graham crackers in the pantry.

By the time she walked out, Cullen stood by the back door with his topcoat in his hands. Not wanting him to leave with her refusal to talk hanging in the air between them, she took them back to neutral conversational ground. "Thanks again for your help."

Shrugging into his overcoat, he nodded. "It's not a problem."

His voice was gruff, as if her refusal to talk had annoyed him, so she smiled and said, "Still, it's very kind of you to be so good to Harry."

"I'm good to Harry because I like him." He spoke softly, and Wendy quickly glanced over at him. "I like you both."

His unexpected statement left Wendy with no chance to stop her automatic response to it. Her cheeks flushed. The air in the room evaporated. Joy coursed through her veins. All of which was ridiculous. They could not have a relationship. She shouldn't even *want* a relationship with a playboy who would disappear from her life when his work in Barrington was done. But with Harry in the picture, it was doubly wrong.

She quickly turned to the sink again, grabbed a paper towel from the wall-mounted roller and dried her hands. Keeping her voice light and friendly, she said, "We like you, too."

She heard him take the few steps to the counter and wasn't surprised when she felt his hands on her shoulders, or that he turned her to face him. "No. I mean I really like you. I feel so at home here."

Not knowing whether to be relieved or disappointed, Wendy laughed. "You *lived* here. Of course, you feel at home here."

He shook his head. "This was hardly a home. My parents were rarely around. Which was actually good because when they were here they fought."

"Your parents fought in front of you?"

"They weren't much on the decorum of fighting." He took a breath, as if he couldn't believe he'd actually admitted that. "My dad wanted to leave Barrington. He knew he could start an investment firm anywhere. But my mom didn't want to leave her friends. The people who depended on her for their jobs."

Wendy's eyes widened. "That's why you didn't want to go into the plant alone?"

"No. I've simply never been on the plant floor before. I didn't know anyone and I didn't want to scare anyone. The first morning, when I saw everybody peeking into your office to say good morning in the few minutes before you came into my office to explain why you were late, I knew you were the perfect person to introduce me around."

That made sense, but she suddenly realized they were standing close, his hands still on her shoulders. Memories of their kiss came tiptoeing back, causing her lips to tingle and her breathing to falter. He was the first man to kiss her since Greg. She'd been alone so long. Empty for so long—

Neither of which made wanting him right. Especially when he was so wrong for her.

She cleared her throat. "I guess I'd better finish cleaning up so I can get up on time for Harry tomorrow."

He grinned. "You slept in? That's why you were late Monday morning?"

"It wasn't funny. I'm trying to be a good parent to Harry, and the very first time he was supposed to be somewhere I slept in."

"Oh, Wendy," he said, wrapping his arms around her and pulling her close. "You are only human."

The feeling of being held by a man flooded her system. The joy of the emotional connection with someone who seemed genuinely to like and understand her nearly overwhelmed her. Then the scent of his aftershave filtered to her and she realized her breasts were nestled against his chest. Their thighs brushed. Strong muscles braced her softer form. They fitted together perfectly. And she so wanted to fit with someone again.

She took a breath to bring herself back to reality. She and

Cullen *didn't* fit. He was a playboy. She wouldn't get involved with a man who wouldn't be interested in anything permanent. By Christmas day he'd be gone. If she depended upon him too much, grew accustomed to having him around, or, God forbid, actually fell in love with him, she'd find herself with a broken heart on Christmas morning.

She pulled herself out of Cullen's warm embrace. "Thanks for your help tonight." She motioned to the door. "I'll see you on Monday."

Time suspended for the few seconds it took for Cullen to get her message. It looked as if he might say something, then he turned on his heel and headed for the door. "Good night, Wendy."

"Good night, Cullen."

She said the words softly, but it really didn't matter. He'd already walked out and closed the door. The soft click echoed through her empty kitchen.

Busying herself with finishing the dishes, she ignored the emptiness. She was glad he could help her through some of the initial difficulties with Harry. She wasn't too proud to refuse the assistance that a scared little boy needed. But she was also smart enough not to get sucked into the daydream that she might be the woman to tame the playboy who owned the company where she worked. She was even smarter not to get involved with another man who would dictate, not discuss. She'd been hurt once and she wouldn't let it happen again. She had everything she wanted now. A child. And she would never risk hurting Harry.

She dried her hands on a paper towel and threw it in the trash before heading for bed. If she was so smart and had done all the right things, why the hell was she so damned disappointed that he hadn't argued, but had simply gone?

Which proved she really didn't mean anything to him.

CHAPTER SIX

CULLEN just barely caught his flight to Miami. Exhausted from the week of almost nonstop work, he fell asleep two minutes after takeoff, and woke when the wheels touched down at Miami International. But part of him was glad. He'd never felt as odd as when Wendy showed him the door that night. She'd kicked him out. *Out.* After he'd helped her! And told her the thing about his parents that he'd never told anyone. That they fought. Often. If he'd stayed awake, he would have spent the entire flight fuming about that.

Hoisting his duffel bag off the carousel in baggage claim, echoes of the odd sensations he'd felt when she pointed at her kitchen door rumbled through him again. He reminded himself that he had already been in his coat and she probably had been tired. Walking out into the balmy Miami night, he decided that she hadn't so much kicked him out as gotten him moving.

In his Mercedes, he lowered the convertible top and exited the airport, letting the wind whip through his hair as he made his way to the house on the beach that he shared with his dad.

But he couldn't stop thinking about Wendy, about how the emotion of the situation had caused him to hug her and her to cuddle into his embrace. What he'd felt in those few seconds was different than anything he'd ever felt with a woman.

He frowned. Maybe *different* wasn't the right word. *Expanded* was better. He felt all the usual male/female things he felt when he held a woman, but there was more.

Over an icy weekend, they'd both helped Harry adjust to living with her. She'd told him bits and pieces of her life. He'd told her bits and pieces of his. Together they'd told Harry about his dad, then helped him get through the difficult evening with hot dogs and s'mores.

Of course he felt close to her. He typically didn't get this involved in *anybody's* personal life. When he pulled her into his arms, he wasn't simply wooing an attractive woman, he was holding somebody he knew. Somebody he liked. The velvet of her skin was warm and familiar. The questions in her eyes echoed his own. In a few short visits, they'd become so close that he swore he could feel her heart beating.

Then she'd kicked him out.

With a growl of annoyance, he reminded himself he'd already figured out that she'd done it because she was tired, but he suddenly realized that wasn't what bothered him. The real problem wasn't being "kicked out." It was being kicked out after her refusal to talk about her husband.

Driving along the coastal highway, wind in his hair, the perfect world around him glittering with lights, the ocean a peaceful rumble to his left, he wondered if she hadn't kicked him out *because* he'd asked about the picture. Which was really rich since *he* was the one who had the right to be insulted. It had been years since her husband's death and his question had been innocent, yet she wouldn't answer it. He'd automatically told her things about his family. He'd answered every damned question she'd asked him. But she didn't want to talk about her husband.

He slapped his hand on the steering wheel. Damn it! What did it matter? He'd never pursue her. She was a serious woman and he was a flirt. A guy who liked to have fun. Were it not for Harry, they'd probably never even speak outside the office.

Maneuvering his car onto the driveway that led to his rambling two-story stucco house with windows that rose to the sky, Cullen told himself to relax. Really relax or his dad would figure out something was wrong and wouldn't let Cullen rest until Cullen spilled the whole story. And then his dad would be angry. He'd think that Barrington, Pennsylvania, was sucking Cullen in the way it had his mom. The memories that would be dredged up would ruin Christmas. So, no. He absolutely, positively would not let on that anything was bothering him.

Because nothing *was* bothering him. He accepted that Wendy didn't want to talk about herself. It was just another proof that he and his family didn't fit into the town that bore their name. He didn't know why he'd been so foolish as to think Wendy might be different, but he'd gotten the message. From here on out he wouldn't ask her questions about her life and he'd keep his own life off-limits, too.

The house was dark and quiet when he entered the echoing foyer. Assuming his dad was asleep, and without turning on a light, he carried his duffel bag up the curving cherrywood stairway and walked down the hall to his suite of rooms. He was determined to forget all about Wendy Winston and Harry Martin and spend Saturday and Sunday enjoying himself on his boat, soaking up the sun before he had to fly back to frosty Barrington on Monday afternoon.

Wendy let Harry sleep in on Saturday morning. When eleven o'clock came and went with Harry still asleep, she cancelled her plans with Emma and her kids. He woke about noon, sullen and cranky, and Wendy gave him a lot of leeway, letting him work out his feelings in his own way. On Sunday when he was still moody, she ordered pizza and let him watch football on television. But Monday morning when he refused to go to school, she knew he had to snap out of this.

She took a firm hand and got him dressed and fed him. After she walked him to his class, she explained his situation to his teacher, then spent another few minutes in the principal's office, telling the story again, making sure Harry would have sufficient support.

She arrived at work over an hour late, only to discover Cullen wasn't there. Breathing a sigh of relief, she got busy with her typical Monday-morning duties and forgot all about her temporary boss.

When Cullen hadn't arrived at noon, she took her lunch, expecting him to be in Mr. McCoy's office when she returned, but he wasn't. Worried now, she called his hotel and discovered he'd checked out. Assuming he'd gone to Miami for the weekend, she relaxed, until another hour went by. If he had no intention of returning until Tuesday, he should have let her know. She was, after all, his assistant. She scoured her desk for a note, then scoured his. Nothing.

At three, she began to fear that maybe something had happened. He could have been in an accident. By the time he strolled into her office after four, every nerve ending in her body was sitting on the edge of her skin like glitter.

"Where were you?"

His eyebrows rose at her tone. "Excuse me?"

She combed her fingers through her hair. "Sorry. I had a bad weekend and when you weren't here and there wasn't a note—" She fisted her hair in her hands this time. "I just panicked and thought you must have been in an accident. I'm sorry."

He shucked his overcoat. "No. I'm sorry. You're right. I should have let you know I would be going home for weekends and not returning until late Monday."

"It's almost quitting time. You shouldn't have bothered to come in at all."

He laughed. "You *are* in a mood."

She sighed. "Harry had a bad weekend."

"I'm not surprised. He lost his mom and spent a month in foster care. When he was finally given to you—someone he knew and felt safe with—he was told his dad was dead."

His instant understanding made her so damned glad to see him that she was sure it showed on her face. They might be different. They might even be unsuited. But he absolutely understood her and what she was going through with Harry.

She busied herself stacking the pages she'd just pulled from the printer, turning her face away so he couldn't read anything into her expression. "It has been an awful month for Harry."

"My offer of dinner is still open. Remember, I promised Randy that I'd look in on you."

"And you can. But I—" She glanced over and totally lost her train of thought. He always looked positively yummy, but two days in the sun had given his skin a warm glow. He looked rested, relaxed and so damned sexy that her heart skipped a beat. Her own skin flushed with color but not from the sun, from being flustered and tongue-tied. God, she was an idiot. Not just attracted to a man who was out of her league, but also unable to hide it.

"I—"

His eyes narrowed. "You what?"

She pulled in a breath that caused her breasts to swell beneath her warm pink sweater and Cullen suddenly realized what was going on. She hadn't kicked him out of her house on Friday because she was moody or tired or even unwilling to talk about her husband. She *liked* him. He'd worried all damned weekend for nothing.

He grinned. "You want to orchestrate my visits, don't you?"

She wouldn't look at him again. "I just want to make sure that you're not around so much that Harry misses you when your work here is done."

He stepped closer. "Ah."

"Now you're making fun of me."

He slid his index finger under her chin and lifted her face so that she would look at him. "No, I'm just curious about why you're afraid of me."

"I'm not afraid of you."

"Of course you are," he said, holding her gaze, noting that her pretty green eyes had flecks of gold and that her skin was a smooth, perfect pink.

He gave her points for not yanking herself away from him and breaking eye contact, even as he wondered why he was forcing himself into a situation that was totally wrong. He knew as well as she did that two people who were this attracted couldn't have a lot of contact or they'd spontaneously combust one day and do something they'd both regret. Yet here he was, pushing.

"Or I could simply be too busy with Harry to add another thing to my life."

Her gaze flicked down for a mere second as she said that and he knew that if she wasn't out-and-out lying, she was at least only telling him a half truth.

Before he could stop himself or once again remind himself of all the reasons he shouldn't be insinuating himself into her life, he said, "We both know this isn't completely about Harry, so why don't you tell me what's really going on? On Friday night you were fine and then suddenly you kicked me out. Let's start there."

She pulled away from him and rounded her desk so she could stand behind it, almost as if she wanted protection. "You're a playboy. Anything between us would mean very little to you. But even if you weren't, you're too much like my husband."

He'd been all ready to argue her concerns about him being a playboy until she mentioned her husband. "What?"

"You're like my husband. Greg was a wonderful person. And he always seemed to know the right thing to say…the right thing to do. So much so that I never argued when he made all our decisions." She finally glanced up from the papers she was stacking. "That cost me the chance to have a child of my own with him. Had I pushed for the one thing I truly wanted, a baby, I wouldn't have been alone when he died. I would have also proven myself a capable parent. Nobody would wonder whether I could care for Harry."

This time Cullen took the step back. "You're saying you don't want me around me because I'm like your husband?"

She raked her fingers through her hair. "Yes. No. Because for me this isn't about you and me. It can't be. It has to be about Harry."

"Why?"

"You don't think he'll miss you when you return to Miami?"

And suddenly he got it. They were talking about Harry, but she was also talking about herself. *She* would be hurt when he left. *She* would miss him.

He took another step back. Away from her. The events from Friday night came back to him in a rush. He couldn't help himself from being romantic with her, from touching her, from wanting to kiss her again. Now, she was telling him she didn't want to be involved with him because he reminded her of her husband. Which should—and did—put the appropriate fear in him. Tighten his chest. Make his heart speed up and his stomach tighten. *She was seeing him as a husband.*

And he was a bachelor. She'd even gone so far as to accuse him of being a playboy. He liked Miami. He loved nightlife. He wasn't wild about responsibility so he chose his responsibilities carefully.

But the way he was behaving around her reminded her of a husband.

He took another step back. "I'm helping Harry through a tough time in his life. He needs me because he knows I understand him because my mother also died recently. But by the time I leave, he'll be adjusted to you, secure with you. He'll miss me a bit, but not for long."

"Really?"

The trust in her eyes nearly was his undoing. No one had ever looked at him like that.

He pulled in a breath. Took another step back. He'd never *wanted* anyone to look at him like that.

"Take it from a guy who had to get adjusted to a lot as a kid. Once Harry feels secure with you, I could fall off the face of the earth and he'd be okay in a day or two. It's in this transition time as he's adjusting to living with you that he needs someone he thinks understands, and that's why I'm making myself available."

She smiled and nodded, and Cullen turned on his heel, eager to escape to Paul McCoy's office, but he stopped and faced her again.

"For the record, I would never deliberately hurt anyone."

It was as close as he could come to telling her that he understood her fears. She didn't want his advances, didn't want to get too close because she would be hurt when he left.

He got it.

Now he just had to stop himself from acting on all the impulses that raced through him whenever she was around.

Harry's mood improved greatly on Tuesday morning. Wendy made him oatmeal, sprinkled it with cinnamon and sugar and promised him a trip to the mall after school. She didn't downplay his sadness or his fear of being alone, but rather, tried to show him he was secure with her by feeding him and taking him to school. She promised him the trip to the mall to demonstrate that life went on by making plans for the future.

Walking into work, on time, she experienced a swell of pride until she glanced into Cullen's office and saw him sitting behind Mr. McCoy's big desk.

She knew she'd scared him silly the day before by telling him he reminded her of her husband. She'd done it on purpose. He liked her. She liked him. Their chemistry could go off the charts if they let it, and he didn't seem to have a practicality switch or understand that they were opposites. He might be the if-it-feels-good-do-it type, but she wasn't. If they got involved, he'd have a good time, maybe be sad when he returned to sunny Miami, but in twenty minutes on his boat he'd forget all about her. While she'd be left in snowy Pennsylvania with a broken heart.

No thanks.

She understood that Cullen being in Harry's life in Harry's time of trouble was a good thing. She also got Cullen's point that by the time he left Pennsylvania, Harry would be adjusted. Though he'd miss Cullen, he wouldn't pine for him because he'd be secure with Wendy by then. So it was good for Cullen to be involved with Harry. His point had been made. But she'd also made her point with him. He had to stop giving in to their attraction.

She didn't even poke her head into his office to say good morning. Instead, she stripped off her coat, hung it in the small closet, and went straight to work. A half hour later, he strolled out of his office and stopped in surprise. "Oh, you're here."

She smiled her best administrative-assistant smile. Friendly, but not personal. "I've been here a while."

He angled his hip on her desk and made himself comfortable. "So everything went well this morning?"

"Yes. Harry's back to being his typical sunny self." She pushed her chair back, rose and took some papers to the filing cabinet, putting some distance between them.

"That didn't take long."

Deliberately occupied with filing so she wouldn't look at him, she said, "As you said, he's becoming secure with me."

"You sound like the girl giving the morning news when you talk like this."

"Really?"

Cullen was about to say yes, but he stopped himself. *This* was the reason she would miss him when he left. Because of one icy night together they'd bonded enough that making conversation came naturally. Easily. And, for two people totally unsuited to each other, they really were beginning to like each other too much. He'd already decided to rein in his romantic impulses, but he now saw the reining had to include private conversations.

Without replying, he returned to Paul McCoy's desk. He tried to read the numbers on the production reports, but he couldn't focus, and soon they blurred on the sheet in front of him. Before he knew it, he was thinking about how nice Wendy looked in her blue sweater. With a growl of annoyance, he rose and walked to the window, shifting his thoughts in a direction they were allowed to go: Harry. But thoughts of Harry naturally segued to Wendy again.

He glanced out at her. She sat at her desk diligently typing on her computer keyboard. She'd make a terrific mom, and that made his heart swell with respect for her. He liked Harry. In fact, he saw a little bit of his own loneliness and insecurity as a child when he looked at Harry. Knowing exactly how Harry felt, if he had one wish, it would be that Harry could feel safe and secure. Always. For the rest of his life.

He turned back to the window. He didn't trust wishes. He trusted in his own abilities. Even as a child, he'd quickly realized the only person he could count on was himself. So if he wanted to help Harry, it couldn't be with a wish. It would have to be with something substantial he could do—

Returning to his desk, he grabbed the phone and punched the intercom numbers for the human resources director. There *was* something he could do. And that something might even be why fate had brought him to Barrington.

When Poppy Fornwalt answered her phone, Cullen said simply, "I want the detailed wage reports for the past six months."

Wednesday morning, Harry dressed himself for school and had toast ready for Wendy when she ambled into the kitchen. Pleased, thinking her life was finally settling into a routine, she hugged him and he proudly served her toast with strawberry jam.

Off in her own little world, contemplating how great life would be now for both her and Harry, she drove to work and was surprised out of her reverie when Poppy Fornwalt called her down to her office.

She entered with an enthusiastic hello, and dark-haired, blue-eyed Poppy looked up with a smile. "Close the door."

Wendy swallowed. "You don't normally ask anybody to close the door unless it's bad news," she said, as she pulled the office door shut behind her.

"Or unless we're going to talk money."

She took the seat in front of Poppy's desk. "Money?"

"You really must have impressed Mr. Barrington."

Her eyebrows rose. "Impressed Mr. Barrington?"

"He's giving you a twenty-five percent raise!" Poppy all but bounced out of her seat with joy.

Wendy's mouth fell open. "Twenty-five percent?"

"Yes!" Poppy cried. "And isn't it wonderful timing? He wants it backdated to last week so you'll have extra money in time for Christmas!"

Her heart sank and the world spun, as her head filled with a truly awful conclusion. She'd brushed him off, so he was offering her money? This time her stomach turned over. Was he trying to buy her with a raise? "Oh really."

Poppy's happy expression faded. "You should be dancing.'

Wendy pulled in a breath, working to react naturally to what appeared to be good news, but what was, in reality, the worst possible news. "I'm dancing on the inside."

"Wendy, everybody knows you recently got custody o your neighbor's little boy. Maybe this is his way of helping.'

Wendy forced a smile. "I'm sure it is."

Poppy handed some forms across the desk. "Here's your pa perwork. It has all the numbers. Your raise will be on this pay Mr. Barrington simply asked that we keep this between us."

Wendy rose. "I'm sure he did."

Poppy apparently didn't catch the note of dismay in Wendy's voice because she rose, grabbed Wendy's hand

and squeezed it. "I'm so hoping this helps you with your little boy."

Wendy smiled. She would look incredibly ungrateful if she didn't show some appreciation. "It will. Thank you, Poppy."

"Don't thank me. Thank Mr. Barrington."

"Oh, I will."

Wendy left Poppy's office, not sure if she was furious or ashamed. Particularly since the Barringtons had held raises to cost-of-living raises for the past five years. Being singled out to get a raise when everybody in the plant needed and deserved one, only made Cullen's generosity stand out all the more. If anyone heard about this she'd be a pariah.

By the time she reached her office, she was breathing heavily. She stormed through the open door, into Cullen's office and slapped the paperwork for her raise on his desk.

"What is this?"

He glanced up, took in her angry expression and his brow furrowed. "It's paperwork to give you a raise?"

"I know!" Tossing her arms in the air, she pivoted away from the desk.

"And yet you're angry."

She spun to face him. "What do you think that money is going to get you?"

"Get me?"

"Do you think I'm going to sleep with you for this?"

The expression in his eyes went from confused to fiery in the beat of her heart. "You'd better stop talking and let me explain." Real menace dripped from his words.

Her blood ran cold at his tone. Dear God, he was the boss! He could fire her, call security and have her escorted off the property. And she had a child to think about!

"I checked into your salary to see if I could help you out

since you now have a son to support." He sat back in his chair, tossed his pencil to his desk. "I certainly wasn't intending to pay you to sleep with me."

Her cheeks flamed. The room spun. It was so hard to breathe she wasn't even sure she could speak, but there was no turning back. "You're still treating me differently, showing me favoritism. Even if I was wrong about the reason—" she swallowed "—you can't give me and no one else a raise without making it look like I did something to get on your good side."

"When I checked your salary I saw everybody's. No one in this plant has gotten above a cost-of-living raise in five years. Which is why everybody will be getting a raise similar to yours in January."

Embarrassment coursed through her. She wanted to faint or die, but knew she couldn't do either. She fell to the seat in front of his desk. "Everybody?"

"Yes. When I saw those numbers I was actually glad I was forced to take a real look at what was going on here. My dad and I check the big-picture figures when we get our profits every quarter, but we never looked at the details. Your situation forced me to do that."

"Oh, God." She squeezed her eyes shut.

"You don't trust me. I get it. Personally, man to woman, I'm not to be trusted. I'm not looking for what you want. You probably couldn't live the way I live. But don't ever question my business judgment again."

She swallowed. "I'm sorry."

He sat back on Paul McCoy's tall-backed black leather chair. "I'm not going to tell you it's okay because it isn't. But I am willing to forget about it and move on."

"Thank you."

"And don't tell anyone about the raises."

She looked up, confused.

"You need yours now. Don't tell me you don't. But accounting and human resources need time to process everyone else's. So, on my order, they did yours now. But I don't want anyone to be offended or upset. So please, keep this all under your hat until everyone's raise is announced in January."

She frowned. "But then no one will know you're the one who authorized the raises."

He picked up his pencil and glanced down at the papers in front of him again. "There's no point."

"Sure there is. It's Mr. McCoy who's run such a tight ship that we only got cost-of-living raises. He claimed the plant couldn't afford more. So when he gets back, he'll get the credit for giving everyone their raise."

"This isn't about who gets credit." He didn't even look up. "I was only giving you what you had worked for over the past four years. You may go now."

Dismissed, Wendy rose. She'd put the last nail in the coffin of their friendship, and felt like a complete fool.

CHAPTER SEVEN

THAT night, after tucking Harry beneath a soft comforter and kissing him goodnight, Wendy ambled into her living room. In need of a little comfort herself, she made a fire in the fireplace, found a book and curled up on her sofa.

She read for only twenty minutes before the events of the day weighed down on her. She hadn't meant to insult Cullen. She'd thought she was protecting herself. Which was just more proof that they were too different to get involved. So different she'd seen his kindness as an attempt to buy her favors and embarrassed herself.

Wondering what he saw when he looked at her, at her life, she glanced around his former home. Her sofa and chair were simple beige. The area rug atop the hardwood floors she and Greg had refinished was a modern print in soft yellow, cream and green that brought the room to life. The walls had been painted a pale yellow.

It was a soothing room, a calm room, but it wasn't elegant. She couldn't even imagine the kind of home he lived in in Miami. But he hadn't looked down on her or her things the Saturday he'd stayed with her. He'd joined in her fun with Harry, working to make Harry happy. He'd slept on the floor without complaint and even cooked for her and Harry.

She frowned. Technically, with the exception of kissing her, everything he'd done had been for Harry. When he'd stepped into the conversation with Randy Zamias, when he'd said they shouldn't wait to tell Harry his father had passed, when he'd volunteered to take them out to dinner—all those things had been for Harry. And maybe he hadn't been pushy or domineering, simply desperate to help? As out of his element with the little boy as Wendy had been, he'd made a few mistakes.

So had she.

Yet she'd taken everything personally. Forgetting, or maybe not even noticing, that at the office and in their private conversations, he'd always been a perfect gentleman.

Running her hands down her face in misery, she rose from the sofa to make a cup of hot cocoa, but a blood-curdling scream sounded from upstairs. She dropped her book to the coffee table, raced upstairs and burst into Harry's room.

Sitting in the center of the bed, Harry sobbed. He wasn't wearing his glasses and she could see the tears that poured down his cheeks. She sat on the edge of his bed and he leaped into her open arms.

"It's all right. It's all right."

Sobs racked his small frame and he clung to her. "No, it's not!"

"Did you have a nightmare?"

"Yes."

"Well, I'm here now. You're safe."

"I want Cullen."

Surprised, she pulled in a breath. Not only did it sting that her comfort wasn't enough, but also she wasn't really sure Cullen would come. "It's late. He's at his hotel."

"He said if I ever needed him I could call."

"I'm sure he meant it but it's—"

"I want Cullen!"

He clutched her upper arms tighter and pressed his face in her shoulder, his tears wetting her T-shirt.

Wendy stroked his soft hair. She had to at least try. "All right. I'll call him."

Cullen didn't ask for details. Hearing Harry had had a nightmare and was inconsolable, he raced to Wendy's house. She opened the door before he even knocked. She didn't mention their argument. He didn't either. What happened between them was between them. What happened with Harry wasn't just separate, at the moment it was the only thing that mattered.

"How is he?"

As she led him up the stairs, Wendy said, "Once I called you he stopped crying. So it must have been the right thing to do."

"Let me see what's going on."

He stepped into the little room that had been his own when he and his parents had lived in the house. The bright-blue walls he remembered had been repainted a soothing blue. Trains and dump trucks decorated the comforter. The base of the lamp was in the shape of a football.

Sitting up on the bed, partially covered by the thick blanket and sliding a small plastic car on his thigh, Harry said, "Hi, Cullen."

He sat on the bed. "Hey." He ruffled Harry's hair. "What's wrong?"

Without looking up, he said, "I had a nightmare."

"What kind of a nightmare?"

Harry shrugged.

"Monsters?"

He glanced up. "No."

"Then what?"

"Kids at school."

"Are the kids at school bothering you?"

He shrugged again. "Some."

"Just some?"

"Just one."

"Who is that?"

"Freddie."

"Is he hurting you?"

"No. He just told me I was an organ and nobody wanted me."

Not feeling the need to tell him *organ* was probably *orphan*, Cullen reached over and hugged Harry, then drew him onto his lap. "Wendy wants you so much that she was willing to go to court for you. Why do you think Randy Zamias gives your mom so much trouble?"

Standing just outside the doorway, Wendy leaned against the wall. She wondered if Cullen had slipped up in calling her Harry's mom, but doubted it. He was a very smart guy. He realized Harry needed reassurance, continuity and he was giving it to him in the most subtle way.

Harry twisted to look up into Cullen's face. "Because he wants me?"

"No. Because he needed to be sure the right person has you."

Running the car up his pajama-clad thigh, Harry said, "Did kids tease you when you were in school?"

Watching Cullen's facial features harden, Wendy's brow furrowed. She'd never considered what it might have been like for him to live in the town where his dad's grandparents started the company that provided jobs for nearly everyone in town and his mom was the president who ran it. But it must not have been a joyful experience. Otherwise, his expression wouldn't have gone from sympathetic to hard in an automatic reaction he hadn't had time to stop.

Thinking back to his first day at the plant, she remembered that he wouldn't go onto the plant floor without introductions and none of the employees had treated him normally. Men had grunted hellos. Women had giggled.

Wendy had treated him normally, but only because he'd stayed at her house the night of the ice storm. And she wasn't from Barrington. She'd only moved here four years ago. She had no idea how he'd been treated as a child.

"Yes, kids teased me. But not for the reasons you think. My mom was sort of everybody's boss. When I got into third grade, the kids thought it would be cool to hit me and stuff."

Wendy smiled at the way he brought the language of his conversation to Harry's level.

"Our neighbor down the street, my dad's partner in the candy store, waited for me one day after school and set them straight."

Harry's eyes widened. "He did?"

"Yep. He handed me a brand-new ball and bat, with nine mitts. Enough for an entire team."

"Wow."

"Then he told the kids who'd gathered around us that if we wanted to become a Little League team he would coach us."

"Wow."

Cullen laughed. "He'd coached his own kids, but they'd outgrown Little League and he hadn't."

Wendy tilted her head to the side as a clear image of that day formed in her head. She could see eight-year-old Cullen being teased and tormented, and a family friend stepping in to help him because apparently neither of his parents had noticed.

A shudder of sadness passed through her. He'd been as alone as Harry. But he probably hadn't been an easy mark.

She couldn't imagine that even as a child he'd let anybody push him around, but she also knew most children weren't equipped to defend themselves against a gang.

A sudden realization swamped her. He'd spent most of his life in this town alone, a child constantly being forced to prove himself. Only she had treated him normally. Until Friday night when he had asked about her husband and tried to kiss her a second time, then everything had changed. She'd put her back up and refused to talk, wanting to protect herself. But even though she had explained that, she had nonetheless become another person from Barrington who treated him coolly. Then she'd made the ultimate mistake by accusing him of trying to buy her. Lord, could she have been any more wrong?

Harry shook his head. "Freddie already has a mitt."

"And you don't need to buy gifts to make friends. You said only he teases you. Do the other kids like you?"

He nodded.

"Then you're just going to have to ignore Freddie."

Glad he hadn't told Harry to punch Freddie, Wendy breathed a sigh of relief. Fighting wasn't the answer. But she also wouldn't let Freddie get off scot-free. She'd have a discussion with the principal in the morning.

Harry began rolling the little car along his thigh again. "Do you miss your mom?"

"Sure. But not the same way you do. I don't need my mom to take care of me. You do. So part of what you feel is fear. Especially fear of being alone."

He nodded.

"Wendy's not going to leave you alone. All you have to do is believe in her."

Harry looked up. His blue eyes connected with Cullen's

dark ones. The trust that Wendy saw in them nearly stole her breath. "Okay."

"And any time you get afraid, I want you to call me."

"Okay."

"In fact," Cullen said, reaching over, opening the bedside-table drawer and retrieving a pen and a little tablet. "This is my cell phone number."

Harry grinned. "You have a cell phone? Jimmy Johnson has a cell phone."

He placed the tablet and pen on the bedside table. "Well, now you have my number. You can call me any time. Day or night."

They were quiet for several seconds before Cullen said, "Do you think you can sleep now?"

"Yeah."

"I'll tuck you in."

Rather than laying him down, Cullen switched the mood of their discussion by tossing Harry to the bed. The little boy landed in the middle, his head slightly askew on the pillow. He giggled then said, "Thanks, Cullen."

"Hey, any time."

Cullen pulled the covers to Harry's chin, kissed his cheek and ruffled his hair. "Go to sleep now."

"Okay."

"Okay."

Wendy ducked out of the doorway before Cullen turned in her direction. She raced down the steps as quietly as possible, ran into the living room and fell to her couch, not wanting Cullen to know she'd listened in.

A few seconds later he appeared at the doorway. "I think I have him settled."

"Thank you."

"He only wanted reassurance that everything's going to be

okay." He rolled his shoulders, as if to loosen their tightness. "I gave him my cell phone number."

"You didn't have to do that."

"I don't think he'll bother me. He's in school all day so he doesn't have a lot of access to a phone. Even after school he's with a babysitter until you get home." He met her gaze. "But if he wants to call me forty-six times a day until he's comfortable, I can handle it."

She smiled slightly, feeling like a real jerk for being so wrong about him. "Thanks."

"You're welcome." He turned and walked into the foyer. Wendy scrambled from the sofa and to the door before he opened it.

"I know this was a huge imposition, so I appreciate it."

"Again, you're welcome."

The foyer became quiet. Wendy searched her brain for something to say, but there was nothing, unless she wanted to apologize once more for misunderstanding about the raise. And she didn't care to bring up that particular misery again.

Not sure what else to do, she looked up and found him staring at her, studying her.

She knew he was probably wondering how she could be so dense, and she shook her head. "Look, for two people who got off on the right foot, I know I've made a real mess of things."

"It's okay."

"No, it isn't. You've been nothing but nice to both me and Harry and I've been…well…odd." She pulled in a breath. "You're not like my husband. Not that he didn't have his good points, but when he died, leaving me alone, I got angry. I obviously jumped to some wrong conclusions about you and I'm sorry. I don't normally take that anger out on people."

"But it made you cautious."

She nodded.

"Maybe you *should* be cautious."

She smiled. "Are you warning me off?"

"Yes."

The seriousness of his voice caused her stomach to tighten. She caught his gaze again. His dark eyes virtually glowed, sending a sizzle of electricity through her. If she touched him, she had the feeling he'd be lost.

"I'm not the kind of guy to settle down and you are absolutely the kind of woman to settle down. Even if you didn't have Harry, I would know it. But that doesn't stop me from wanting you. And you're not too far off the mark about me being pushy. When I want something I go after it. And right now I want you."

She licked her lips at the severity of his tone and took a step back.

"Forget all about your first impression and stick with the worry that I'm enough like your husband that you shouldn't get involved with me. We'll both be happier, if only because you don't want to get hurt and I don't want to hurt you."

Swallowing, she caught his gaze. "You don't have to warn me. I can take care of myself. I'm a big girl."

"Not big enough to play in my league."

With that he turned and walked out of her house. Wendy stood in her foyer a long time, every cell in her body tingling. Not just because he was an attractive man, but because he'd admitted that he was so attracted to her he was having difficulty stopping himself from doing what he wanted.

She absolutely knew that feeling. Just being in the same room with him made her blood hum in her veins. She hadn't felt this good, this alive, in years. Though the Miss Goody Two-shoes in her told her to back off, the promise in his soft voice and sensual eyes told her not to listen. She wanted this, and for once in her life she didn't want to walk away wishing things could have been different. For once in her life, she'd simply like to enjoy the moment. Do what she wanted to do instead of what she knew was the "right" thing to do. For once in her life she didn't want to be Miss Goody Two-shoes.

But she didn't really know how to be anybody else.

CHAPTER EIGHT

THE next morning, Wendy met Patty and Emma by the time clock. Patty tapped her forearm to catch her attention. "You know, you haven't really spoken much since you got Harry. Everything okay?"

Punching her time card, Emma added, "You didn't bite off more than you can chew with that little boy, did you?"

Wendy gasped. "Oh, no! I love everything about having Harry in my life."

"Then what?" Emma asked.

Wendy licked her suddenly dry lips. Part of the problem she was having with Cullen was that she hadn't talked about any of this with her friends. The only input and opinion she had was her own. Lately, she was beginning to think she wasn't all that smart when it came to men.

Patty growled, "Come on, spill it."

Catching Patty's arm and nodding to Emma, she moved the three of them to a quiet corner. "Okay. The problem is Mr. Barrington."

Both Patty's and Emma's eyebrows rose. "He's a crappy boss?"

"He's a great boss and he's even been helping me with Harry."

"Oh, really?"

"Harry and I met Cullen the Saturday before he took over for Mr. McCoy."

"The day of the ice storm?"

Wendy winced. "The day we lost power."

"Oh, you little devil! He stayed at your house, didn't he?"

"Yes, and that's why Harry got so close to him."

"And you, too?"

She sighed. "And me, too." Glancing around to make sure the hall was clearing and no one could hear, she took her voice down to a whisper. "Last Friday night, he tried to kiss me and—"

Both Emma and Patty's eyes widened.

"—then we had a bit of a disagreement about money. I more or less accused him of trying to buy me."

This time their mouths fell open.

"Girl, when you decide to have a life you pull out all the stops."

"No kidding. The problem is he's a really great guy. And I'm afraid he's never going to speak to me again because— well, I'm an idiot. I keep taking everything he says and does the wrong way." She shook her head. "But I think he's wrong about a few things, too. He says we're not good for each other because he doesn't want to settle down, but I'm not so sure I want to settle down either right now."

Patty gasped. "You want a fling?"

"Maybe."

"So," Emma said, leaning closer, her eyes bright with excitement, her voice a low whisper. "What are you going to do?"

"I don't know."

"Well, I know," Patty said, grabbing Wendy's hand to make sure she paid attention. "You're going to really listen when he talks, stop jumping to conclusions and stop comparing him to Greg."

Wendy winced. "You figured that out."

"Yes."

Patty glanced at the clock on the wall. "Two minutes to get to the wheel." She sighed. "If we had more time I'd give you real advice, because I saw the way he looked at you. For now, just listen—really listen—to what he's saying and take your cue from that. For God's sake, don't push him, but don't miss the obvious."

Deciding that was probably the best course of action, Wendy headed for her office. When she arrived, Cullen was rifling through the file cabinets in front of her desk.

"Good morning."

Without looking away from the files, he said, "Good morning. So, how was Harry this morning?"

Normal conversation. Thank God. This she could handle. "He was great. Happy as a clam. I reminded him to ignore Freddie, and he grinned."

Cullen shook his head with a chuckle. "Kids. They're very resilient."

"I have a feeling Harry has spent a lot of his life accepting things he couldn't change."

"Yeah, me, too." He paused a second then said, "Are you busy today?"

"Just the usual. But my job title is assistant to the president, so if you need me to do something, your work comes first."

He rubbed his hand along the back of his neck. "I don't really have work for you to do. Actually, I have nothing on my calendar today for myself." He caught her gaze. "So I thought maybe you'd come out with me this afternoon and help me choose a gift for Harry for Christmas." He paused.

"The kid's had it so rough the past few months that I want to buy him a great gift. Something that makes him feel special." He paused. "That is, if it's okay with you."

She nearly cursed herself for being such a hard case that he worried it might not be okay for him to buy Harry something for Christmas. "Of course you can buy him a gift!"

"And you'll help me?"

This was her perfect opportunity to fix the mistakes she kept making with him. Away from the office, away from Harry, they could simply be themselves.

"Sure. I'd love to go shopping."

"I understand there's a mall—"

Before she nodded in agreement, a thought struck her. She wasn't the only one who had made some mistakes about Cullen. The employees had been gossiping ever since he arrived and most of what they'd said had been way off base. When they got their big raises in January, she wanted the people in the town to realize Cullen had been the one who saw the problem and rectified it. Since job confidentiality precluded her from telling anyone he, not Mr. McCoy, had instigated the raises, the best way to help everyone figure it out for themselves would be to get him out among the townspeople. Soon they'd see him for the nice guy he was and know he'd been their benefactor.

"The mall's too impersonal. We should stay in town. There are a few small shops that have some interesting gifts." She slid onto her desk chair. "You're very important to Harry. A gift from you should reflect that."

"I was going to get a dump truck."

She laughed. "You can buy him a dump truck. But let's look around town. See what else might strike your fancy."

He pulled in a breath. "Okay."

"Okay."

He turned to go into his office, but she had a second, even better idea. "We could have lunch at the diner first. Kill two birds with one stone."

He faced her with a scowl. "I don't know."

"Why not?"

"I usually go back to my hotel—"

"Really?" She swallowed back the surprise of that and added, "That's quite a drive for lunch. Let me introduce you to the ladies at the diner. They'll take care of you. Then you won't have to go so far every day."

Cullen was suspicious of Wendy's *they'll take care of you* claim until they stepped into the diner. In the years he'd been out of town, it hadn't changed one iota. Heavy-duty floor tiles in pale brown were flecked with enough colors that they didn't show the dirt from the foot traffic. Chocolate-brown stools rimmed a beige counter. Booths of the same chocolate color lined three of the walls. Tables filled in the center space.

But what he'd missed most in the years he'd been away, without even realizing he was missing it, was the smell. The scents of chicken, pie, French fries, hamburgers, butter and cinnamon mixed and mingled and wafted through the seating area.

Waitresses in pink uniforms dashed from table to table and into the kitchen. Dodie, the same cashier/hostess who'd manned the cash register when he and his parents had come here to eat on special occasions still stood behind the counter, her pink uniform stretched around her round tummy.

"Well, as I live and breathe! Cullen Barrington."

"I didn't think you'd recognize me."

Dodie batted a hand. "Handsome devil like you? Are you kidding?"

He laughed.

She grinned, but her smile quickly faded. "I heard about your mom. I'm sorry."

"Thank you."

"How's your old man?"

"He's fine. The warm weather agrees with him."

"Warm weather agrees with all of us." She peered at Wendy. "And don't think I don't see you standing there, missy. How's that new boy of yours?"

Wendy laughed. "He's great."

"You're going to make him a wonderful mother. You don't let social services push you around."

Wendy shook her head. Dodie knew everything. "I won't."

"Good. Find yourselves a seat. I'll send Mercy over to get your orders."

At the booth, Cullen helped Wendy with her coat and hung it on the hook at the end of the booth along with his topcoat. She slid onto one side, he slid onto the other.

Taking a menu from the holder behind the salt and pepper, she said, "I didn't realize you knew Dodie."

He grabbed a menu, too. "Everybody knows Dodie."

She smiled. "And she knows all of us, too."

His eyes on the menu, Cullen said, "That's the one thing about a small town that's good and bad. Everybody knows everything."

"I think it works in our favor more than it works against us."

"Your family didn't own the town's major employer."

"True." She paused when the waitress came over. Cullen deferred to her and she ordered a salad. He ordered a hot roast beef sandwich.

When the waitress left, she picked up the conversation where it had left off. "So, how was it?"

"Living here?"

She shrugged. "Living here. Living with a mom who was company president." She frowned. "Why was she the one running the company? The company was founded by your dad's grandparents. Why didn't your dad take the job?"

"He didn't want it. All along he wanted to hire a competent manager, move south and enjoy life."

"So what happened?"

"He married a local girl. He met my mom his last year in college and it was love at first sight. They kind of got married without really talking about what they wanted out of life."

Though Wendy and her husband had had a good marriage, it was only because she'd never complained when Greg had totally controlled their lives. "I basically did the same thing."

"Then you understand my dad's disappointment when she wouldn't leave her friends."

"She wouldn't leave her friends?"

"She was afraid that an impersonal manager wouldn't treat the people of the town well."

Wendy shrugged. "In a way she was right. Mr. McCoy hasn't given raises in five long years."

"Yeah, but that doesn't change the fact that my father was miserable. So he hid himself in his work. He started an investment company and grew it until my mom retired."

Which was why a neighbor had to coach Cullen's Little League team. His mom felt it her duty to ensure that her friends at the candy factory were treated right, and his dad hid in his work. No wonder Cullen understood Harry's loneliness.

The waitress came with their drinks and silverware, silently set them on the table and left again.

He nodded at Mercy. "She's not much of a talker."

"She's new. And probably afraid of you."

He snorted a laugh. "Right."

"I'm serious. Everybody's afraid of you or suspicious of why you're here. I figured out last night that the way everybody treats you oddly is part of why you don't want to live here."

"No. I don't care what the people of the town think of me. I don't want to live here because I have a life in Miami. A life I love."

A shiver of caution tripped down her spine, reminding her of how different they were; how they wanted different things out of life. Still, worries like those were irrelevant. She already knew their differences. Yet, she still liked him. A lot. She hadn't even been slightly attracted to a man in so long it felt wrong not to follow up on what she felt for Cullen. And if that led to an affair, it led to an affair. She wasn't going to be Miss Goody Two-shoes anymore. But she wouldn't get her heart broken because she'd go in with her eyes open. No expectations.

"All the same, it wouldn't hurt you to spend a little time with the people your company supports."

"Is that what this is all about?" He motioned around the diner. "Getting me out among the people?"

"No. Yes." She winced. "I think you have a poor opinion of them from your childhood and they have a poor opinion of you since nobody got a raise after you took over."

"That was Paul's doing. Once my mom retired, my dad wouldn't let her even peek at the books, afraid she'd become overinvolved again. Paul was making money for us and we chose to let him do whatever he felt necessary. Now that we know he was a little heavy-handed with the employees, we're fixing things."

"*You're* fixing things. Everybody thinks the no-raise policy came from your family and you're the living, breathing person in Barrington getting the blame. You need to get the credit."

He laughed. "Once again, I don't need the credit."

She toyed with her silverware. "Have you ever stopped to think that maybe *they* need you to take the credit?"

His face twisted in confusion. "How's that?"

"Just as Harry needs to learn to trust me, these people who depend on you need to know that you're trustworthy."

Cullen said nothing.

"Do you want them to spend the rest of their lives wondering if they'll have a job next year?"

"Why would they think that?"

"The rumor has run rampant for years that no raises means no profits, which means there's no reason to keep Barrington Candies open."

"Our profits are fabulous! Why do you think we never sold out when we decided to move away?"

She shrugged. "Everybody felt your family was sentimental."

"Wow." He leaned back in his seat. "Nobody ever leaked the numbers?"

She shook her head.

"*You've* seen the financial reports. Are you telling me you've never even tried to reassure your friends that everything was fine?"

"Of course I did. I'd say things like, 'we have nothing to worry about.' But no one believed me." She pointed across the table. "You, they'd believe."

He closed his eyes and puffed out a breath. "I'm really going to have to do this, aren't I?"

She grinned with delight, her confidence in him blooming. "Yes."

"Damn. I'm not much on PR."

"You'll live."

He laughed and opened his eyes just as Mercy arrived with their food. After she set the dishes in front of them, Cullen looked up at her with a smile. "Thank you, Mercy."

She smiled shakily. "You're welcome, Mr. Barrington."

"You can call me Cullen."

Her eyes widened, but she didn't call him Cullen. She said, "Okay," then scurried away.

"How was that?"

"That was a wonderful beginning."

He picked up his fork and dug into his hot roast beef sandwich. "Just so you know—I'm not doing this to get credit for the raises. I'm doing this so people get comfortable with the idea that their jobs aren't going away."

"You won't be sorry."

"I'd better not be."

When they stepped out of the diner, a faint sheen of snow covered the cars parked on Main Street. A light breeze tousled the feathery tinsel wrapped around the streetlights. The silver bells on light poles jingled.

"Where to?"

"We've got three choices. Perry's Toys, Mac's Hardware or Truffles."

Cullen nearly laughed at the thought of Mac's Hardware until he remembered the hardware store had been the best place to buy trains. Then he heard her mention Truffles, the candy store his father half owned. He was a partner with their former neighbor, Jim Edwards, in the store that sold Barrington Candies as well as toys, gifts and greeting cards. Though Cullen had spent many an afternoon trailing behind Jim when he had coached the Little League team, or watching as he arranged toys and candy displays, he hadn't seen Jim in years.

"Let's go to Truffles."

They walked side by side down the sidewalk, passing shops decorated for the holiday with brightly colored lights and tinsel. The airy snow danced around them, as if refusing to fall. The scent of cinnamon and apples wafted from the bakery. He felt the strangest urge to take Wendy's hand and tuck it in the crook of his elbow, but he knew that wasn't only silly, it would start tongues wagging. So he kept his distance, but it didn't feel right. When he was with her he had the oddest urges to protect her from the snow, warm her hands with his own, tell her his deepest, darkest secrets.

All of which were wrong. They were too different to consider their attraction anything more than a potential affair and she wasn't the kind of woman to have affairs, though he knew she was weakening. The night before he'd seen the light in her eyes. They had chemistry stronger than any he'd ever experienced. It was hard enough for him to resist it. Maybe she couldn't. Maybe she didn't want to?

No. He wasn't even going to *think* in that direction. It wasn't right. She would miss him when he returned to Miami, and be hurt that he hadn't even considered staying. And he wouldn't even look back.

When they reached Truffles, he opened the door and a bell jingled.

"Good afternoon, Mr. Edwards," Wendy called.

Cullen stopped just inside the door, memories of his childhood washing over him. The store didn't have typical shelves. Instead, three-tiered tables were arranged around the showroom floor. The bottom tier of the first table held short, cuddly elves. The middle tier had slightly taller Santas. The third tier held a tall music box.

Each table was similarly appointed. Short toys, candy boxes or holiday decorations nestled on the first tier. Taller items sat on the second and the tallest on the third.

Red and green ribbons had been entwined with tinsel and looped along the walls. Holly and evergreen accented with fat red velvet-ribbon bows lined the counter.

The curtain separating the showroom from the storage room slid open and Jim stepped behind the counter, wiping his hands on a red-and-green towel. "Good afternoon, Wendy—"

He stopped, peering through the little round glasses on the end of his nose. "Well, Cullen Barrington! Your dad mentioned you'd be in town."

Cullen stepped over to the counter and shook Jim's hand. Short and bald, wearing a red plaid work shirt and jeans, Jim looked ten years older than Cullen's father, though they were the same age. "Nice to see you, Jim."

"You know the missus will shoot me if I don't ask you to supper tonight."

Cullen patted his tummy. "I'm afraid I had a hot roast beef sandwich at the diner."

Jim laughed. "One day soon then?"

"I'll call Rosie," Cullen promised.

Nodding his agreement, Jim said, "So what can I do for you?"

Wendy said, "Cullen would like to buy Harry a Christmas gift."

"The little boy you brought here the other night?"

She nodded.

Jim brightened, tossed the towel to the counter and came out from behind it. "We have some fabulous gifts for a six-year-old."

As Jim scurried to the front window display, Cullen

watched Wendy's eyes light up. She was so pretty. So innocent. And darned near as easy to please as Harry.

He thought about the last time he'd been shopping. He'd gone to a boutique in Miami, stepped into a room scented with roses, was given a cup of spicy tea and told what he would buy his latest lady friend. Because it was all the rage. Because it had a price so high he wasn't told the price. He didn't see it until he signed his credit-card receipt.

"Here you go."

Jim pulled an old-fashioned fire truck from the display. "He'll love this."

Wendy's mouth fell open in awe. She spun to face Cullen. "Oh, he will! As we were driving to the office the Saturday I got custody, he told me he wanted to be a fireman."

"And it's got a bell," Cullen said, finding a little string tab and tugging twice to make the bell ring. "I don't know what it is with that kid and bells but he loves them."

Wendy laughed. "It's true. When Harry and I walked here the other night, he did nothing but chatter about the bell on Creamsicle's collar."

Cullen stared at her. Mesmerized. Smitten. Her eyes were alight with joy, her cheeks flushed. Her lips plump and kissable. His fingers itched to skim her jaw, tilt her face up for a kiss.

To distract himself, he lifted the little truck to examine it. "It's not very big."

Jim chuckled. "It's a replica of the one we have at the firehouse."

"It's a small-town truck?" Cullen peered at it from all angles. "He'll love it," Jim assured him.

"Okay. I'll take it." He handed the truck to Jim and turned to walk back to the counter. "And don't tell me it's free."

Scurrying behind the cash register, Jim said, "Not on your life! The same rules apply as when you were a kid. Just because your dad owns half this store, that doesn't mean you get everything half off."

Cullen shook his head and turned to Wendy. "My dad had a thing about making me responsible." The second the words were out of his mouth, he snapped it shut. Why did he constantly confess his secrets to her?

"And yet you survived."

And why did her response always make him laugh? Make him feel normal, as if his past was just like anybody else's, riddled with ups and downs that were part of everybody's growth from child to adult?

Jim rang up the sale, telling Cullen a price that caused his eyes to narrow. "I thought you said there was no discount."

"There isn't. That's the price."

Handing his credit card across the counter, Cullen glanced around the store, his gaze automatically finding Wendy. Standing by one of the three-tiered tables, she examined a row of Christmas ornaments, all of which she returned to the display. He took in her serviceable gray wool coat, plain white mittens and simple black boots.

He wondered when she'd last spent money on herself and knew it had probably been a long time ago and even then she'd purchased the sensible items. The mittens that matched every coat or jacket. The boots she could wear everywhere.

He'd love to buy her a fancy coat, leather gloves, high-heel boots to be worn only on special occasions. Without any trouble, he could envision her face lighting up when she opened the packages. She wouldn't fake an "oh" or "ah." Her surprise would be genuine, her pleasure sincere.

The thought filled him with indescribable warmth that

tingled through his bloodstream. Without even closing his eyes he could see them together on Christmas morning. Harry surrounded by wrapping paper. Wendy's face wreathed in smiles. While he sat on the sofa, one arm stretched leisurely across its back, a cup of coffee in his free hand, enjoying the show taking place in front of a sparkling Christmas tree by the crackling fire in the fireplace.

Disappointment that he couldn't be around on Christmas Day brought him back to reality, but he stopped it in its tracks. He was an adult, and he knew the truth about life. A person couldn't have everything he or she wanted. Which was actually good. Because the things we wanted didn't always turn out to be so wonderful. So it was best to hold back. Not wish. Simply accept that our visions of life were always happier than reality.

Still, that didn't mean he couldn't surround Harry with presents and buy as many things as he wanted for Wendy. That was, after all, how he lived. From a distance. He'd buy the gifts, envision their joy and imagine it as he sat on his boat, soaking up the sun, fishing with his dad.

That was reality.

He signed his credit-card receipt, took his package and walked over to Wendy. "Ready?"

She smiled and he smiled, though he knew she hadn't a clue. He would put that smile on her face again on Christmas morning. He might not sit on her sofa and watch, but he would know he had made her smile.

The odd warmth filled him again only this time he recognized it. Contentment. It was as if he'd figured out that the real reason for his trip to Barrington was to meet her and make her happy, and he had zeroed in on how to do it. Finally, finally, he'd figured out why he always had a sense that he was supposed to be around her.

"Ready when you are."

They stepped out into the cool December afternoon and Wendy automatically turned in the direction of the factory again. Cullen caught her arm. He wouldn't risk buying something she didn't want…or even a color she didn't like or a style she didn't care for.

"We're not done yet."

She glanced up at him. "We're not?"

But he also couldn't tell her he was buying her gifts. She'd refuse them before he even had a chance to shop. He had to watch what she paused beside, what she examined, what she sighed over. But he couldn't do that if she wasn't in a store. "Let's spend a little more money on Harry."

"Why? You bought him exactly what he wants. You don't need to spend more."

"I just—"

He stopped. The confused expression on her face banished the warm, fuzzy feeling of contentment. What was he doing? They didn't really have a relationship. He didn't really know her. And as for figuring out that the real purpose of him being in Barrington was to buy her gifts—well, that was idiotic. Gifts, like a raise, could be misconstrued, and hadn't they already had enough trouble because of misunderstandings? She'd warned him off at least twice. He'd warned her off the thought of having a fling the night before. This cat-and-mouse game that continually tried to pull him in was going to get her hurt, and he refused to let that happen.

"No. You're right."

They walked the length of Main Street in silence, the snow swirling around them like ballet dancers enjoying the notes of a perfect song, the scents of pies and cookies enticing them, the low hum of sporadic traffic hardly penetrating his consciousness. Try as he might to keep his distance, he was ultra-aware of Wendy. He wanted to take her hand, enjoy the quiet walk.

He always loved his time with her. Always felt happy, normal and wonderful around her. Which was undoubtedly why he yearned for a kiss. The season was romantic. But his feelings around her and for her were new and special. No one had ever made him feel like this and for that reason alone he'd love to explore whatever it was that hummed between them.

That was the real bottom line. The thing that kept nagging at him. He'd never felt this way about anyone and it seemed wrong not to at least enjoy it while it lasted. This happiness might not be permanent, but she wasn't a child. She was twenty-six. A widow. If she wanted to have a fling, who was he to decide that they shouldn't?

Maybe if he stopped trying to give her gifts to assuage his hunger and was honest with her, they could have something wonderful for the final two weeks he was here?

CHAPTER NINE

"CULLEN?"

Standing on Wendy's front porch, feeling like a gangly teenager who'd finally found the nerve to visit the girl he had a crush on, Cullen had to work to hide his embarrassment. Which was crazy. His relationships were always short-term, for fun. He shouldn't feel any differently just because the woman he was pursuing lived in Pennsylvania.

"Hi. I...um...came to see how Harry is."

The little boy in question appeared from behind Wendy's knees. His wispy yellow hair floated on his forehead to the rim of his glasses. His smile was wide and welcoming.

"Hi, Cullen!"

Wendy stepped aside and invited Cullen into her foyer. "Hi, Harry!" he said, picking up the little boy and looping him over his shoulder.

Harry whooped with delight, and Cullen surreptitiously glanced at Wendy. She didn't seem displeased that he'd come to visit Harry, but he hoped she'd be even more pleased when she realized that the real reason for his visit was to have some alone time with her.

"We were just about to get Harry ready for bed."

Which was exactly why he'd timed his visit for later in the evening.

"Why don't I read Harry his bedtime story?" And after that he and Wendy would be alone and he could either see for himself that she wasn't so nice, so perfect, so wonderful, and that all these emotions swirling around him were ridiculous, or she'd get the message that to him sexual attraction meant exactly that. Sexual attraction. Not love. Certainly not marriage. And they'd get involved. On his terms.

Wendy shrugged. "Sounds good to me." She turned to go up the stairs. Harry followed her. Cullen followed Harry.

Stopping in the hall outside Harry's door, she pointed to the bedroom. "I'll get the bath ready. You two get a clean pair of pj's from his dresser."

Harry obediently walked into his bedroom, directly to the dresser. He opened the drawer, pulled out a pair of pajamas, left the room and headed for the bathroom.

Cullen smiled. That was easy.

Watching through the open bathroom door, he saw Wendy pull off Harry's T-shirt. Over the little boy's head she called, "There are three library books in the bottom drawer of his bedside table. Pick one. He'll be in in a minute."

Cullen went to the bedside table, sat on the bed, and opened the bottom drawer to find three worn children's books. He pulled out the last book, leafed through it to make sure he hadn't made a bad choice and decided he'd be okay with the story about a pig in a puddle.

Tossing the book to the bed, he rose and shrugged out of his leather jacket. He hung it across the back of the chair tucked under a Harry-sized desk and walked to the window.

Outside, the dusting of snow had turned into an inch of fluffy white that sparkled in the streetlights. Car windshields were covered. A coating clung to bare black branches of the big trees in the front yards in Wendy's neighborhood. The quiet, peaceful scene almost made his plans feel all wrong.

Almost.

Small-town women weren't any less sexual than those in the big city. They were simply more discreet, and he could be discreet.

"All set," Wendy said and Cullen turned to see her standing behind Harry who grinned at him.

"I'm all set, too."

"I found a story about a puppy in a puddle."

Harry rolled his eyes. "You mean a pig in a puddle."

Laughing, Cullen walked to the bed. "Same thing."

"No, it isn't!" Harry looked horrified. "There's a big difference between a pig and a puppy."

Struggling with a smile, Wendy grabbed Harry's doorknob as she left the room. "I'll just leave you two alone for now." She closed the door behind her.

Harry scrambled under his covers, took off his glasses and set them on the bedside table. Cullen sat on the bed.

Twenty minutes later, with Harry fast asleep and Cullen's tongue about tied in a knot from all the rhyme and alliteration in the storybook he'd read, Cullen walked down the steps. He casually tossed his jacket over the coat tree in the foyer and walked into the living room where Wendy sat.

Now things would get interesting.

She looked up from the book she was reading. "How did it go?"

"He's out like a light." He casually walked to the sofa and sat beside her. Not so close as to appear inappropriate, not so far away that he wouldn't accomplish his purpose.

"I think I should stay awhile, though, make sure he doesn't have a nightmare and wake up."

She set her book on the coffee table and reached for a round yellow pot. "Hot cocoa. Would you like a cup?"

"Sure."

She poured some into one of the bright yellow mugs on the bamboo tray and handed it to him.

"Smells great." But she smelled even better. The scent of her floated around him. He guessed it was shampoo. Every time she moved, her long red curls danced and shifted, sending the aroma of something light and floral swirling around him. All his hormones cheered. He'd absolutely made the right decision.

"It's from scratch."

"From scratch?"

"I made it myself. I boil cocoa, butter, sugar and vanilla until it makes syrup, then I add whole milk."

He took a sip. "That's really good."

"I don't make it often because it's fattening and probably full of cholesterol."

But tonight was a special night. Damn it. She didn't even have to say the words. He got the message. Because he felt it too, the strange sense of being in the right place at the right time enveloped him. No matter how he tried to keep things purely sexual, something else hummed between them. And that "something else" wasn't what he wanted out of life. He knew that "something else" let people down. He didn't want to be let down the way his parents had been. He didn't want to let Wendy down the way her husband had.

He leaped up off the sofa. "You know what? It's getting late. Harry'll probably be fine." He headed for the door. "I'll see you in the morning."

She rose from the sofa, gave him a confused smile. "Okay."

* * *

Cullen didn't say another word to her. He grabbed his jacket and ran from her house. Wendy dropped her head to her hands. She was such a klutz. A ditz. And the worst of it was, this time she had absolutely no idea what she'd done wrong.

She ambled to bed, miserable.

Friday morning, he barely spoke to her and he left for Miami before noon. Emma and Patty took an early lunch, and Wendy missed them, but she wasn't ready to share anyway. She was growing a tad tired of looking like an idiot. Not just to Cullen, but to her friends.

Saturday morning, Emma and Patty surprised Wendy with an early-morning visit.

Motioning for them to enter her kitchen, she said, "What are you two doing here?"

Emma held up a box of doughnuts. "We've brought food."

"So you'll spill the beans," Patty added as she shrugged out of her coat and hung it on the peg by the door.

Still not quite sure she was ready to talk, Wendy took the box of doughnuts to her kitchen table. "Spill what?"

Patty glanced around. "First of all, where's Harry?"

"Watching cartoons."

"Good."

"Yeah, because now we can get into the juicy stuff." Patty walked to the table. "I saw his car here Thursday night."

Wendy frowned. "What were you doing out in this part of town?"

"Forgot my inhaler at work," Patty said. "Had to call Wendell to let me in."

"Oh."

"So," Emma prodded, sidling up to Wendy as she poured three mugs of coffee. "What happened?"

Wendy glanced over at Emma. "Nothing."

"Oh, come on." Patty sat on one of the chairs at the round kitchen table.

Handing Emma one of the mugs of coffee, Wendy said, "It's true. He came to check on Harry, read him a story, took one sip of the hot cocoa I had made while he was reading and bolted."

"Bolted?" Emma sat beside Patty. "Interesting choice of words."

"Because it's true. He ran as if his feet were on fire."

Patty grinned at Emma. "Very interesting."

"Very embarrassing. I'm guessing the cocoa sucked."

Emma leaned closer to Wendy. "I'm guessing he hadn't come over for cocoa."

Patty leaned in, too. "And you confused him." She shook her head in dismay. "Who offers a man like Cullen Barrington cocoa? It's like saying you're homespun—which means you want a home—which he probably interprets as meaning you want marriage."

Wendy gasped. "I didn't mean that!"

"Of course you didn't." Emma sighed. "You hardly know the man. You shouldn't want to marry him."

Patty shook her head. "You are really rusty."

"Rusty?"

"On dating. Which is why we're here. Monday morning you're not going to look like Suzy Snowflake."

"Or Sandy Secretary," Emma agreed. "He's interested, but you keep confusing him."

"So we're going to help you pick your outfits for next week, so you stop sending mixed signals."

Wendy bit her bottom lip. "I'm not sure this is a good idea."

Both friends put their folded arms on the table. "Why?"

"Because he…he's…"

"Different," Emma supplied. "We get it."

"He's not going to settle down with you." Patty snagged a doughnut. "But you need to get back into the real world."

Emma also took a doughnut. "Consider him practice."

"And if you're lucky, you'll get lots and lots of *practice*."

Wendy hid a shudder of pleasure. She told herself nothing could come of this, but just as quickly reminded herself that Emma was right. Even if nothing happened between her and Cullen, she needed to practice even simple things like how to make small talk, what drinks to serve and even how to dress. She wouldn't make a big deal out of this. She knew the truth. Cullen wasn't the kind to settle down.

But a little voice in her heart reminded her that plenty of flings had turned into the real thing. Practice or not, she liked him. There were so many things to like about him. And maybe…just maybe…

She shoved those thoughts away, telling herself she shouldn't wish for things that couldn't be. But try as she might to think of spending time with Cullen as only a trial run, she liked him. And she could very well end up hurt.

But playing it safe had gotten her hurt, too.

There was no easy answer.

She pulled in a breath. "All right, I'm in. Just don't make me look like somebody I'm not."

Cullen spent the weekend on his boat, soaking in the tropical sun, reminding himself that *this* was where he belonged.

When he returned to Barrington Candies late Monday afternoon, he kept his head down. He plowed through Wendy's office and only grunted hello as he strode by. He even closed the door.

He didn't get involved with women like Wendy. Normally, he didn't even want to. Not because they were somehow wrong, but because he was fair. They were looking for something he couldn't give, so he unselfishly let them alone.

So why the devil couldn't he just do that with Wendy?

He had absolutely no idea, but he did know that his innate sense of fairness would keep him in line. A bit of sexual desire would not be his undoing. He could control the crazy urges he had to touch her and taste her and kiss her. And by God, he would!

After hanging his leather jacket in the closet, he strode to his desk. In keeping with Wendy's suggestion that he behave a little more comfortably with the workers as a subtle reassurance that their jobs were safe, he'd chosen to wear corduroy trousers and a green sweater over a white shirt, and was amazingly comfortable himself. He reminded himself that was because he typically worked in casual trousers and lightweight shirts, in beachfront restaurants or on boats, persuading investors to trust him with their money. He wasn't the kind of guy who liked being stuck in an office—though he couldn't say he'd been unhappy here at Barrington Candies. In fact, he'd been amazingly happy.

He growled at himself. Told himself to stop. One woman couldn't change how he felt about everything in his life!

Tuesday morning, he arrived in the office when Wendy was away from her desk. The minute his butt hit the chair, he put his head down and set his mind on the production figures from the day before. He didn't surface until eleven o'clock, when he needed to see the five-year plan again. Hitting a button on his phone, he buzzed Wendy.

No answer.

He tried again.

No answer.

With an annoyed sigh, he rose and walked into her office

only to find she wasn't there. Thinking she might be in the clerical area, and sorely in need of a short walk to stretch his muscles, he walked out.

Remembering Wendy's suggestion about helping the employees grow accustomed to him, he smiled. "Has anyone seen Wendy?"

A pretty brunette glanced up at him in surprise. "She's on the factory floor, doing a quick safety audit."

"Thanks."

She nodded eagerly, obviously happy to have been called upon.

Cullen headed for the factory floor. He knew that in their small company employees did a lot of double duty. It wasn't a surprise that the employee who probably kept the records for the safety equipment was the one who walked through the plant to make sure everything was where it was supposed to be.

But he really couldn't wait until she was done to get the reports he needed. He opened the door to the plant and the scents of chocolate and peanut butter that had floated on the air all morning hit him in earnest, making his mouth water. But he forgot all about the sweet temptation when he saw Wendy at the other end of the floor.

Wearing a black skirt and crisp white blouse, she looked coolly efficient. That thought registered and then floated away when his eyes ran the length of exposed leg. He'd never seen her legs before. Realizing he was staring, he gave himself a mental shake and began walking toward her.

For Pete's sake, he partied with women in thong bikinis! How could he be so startled, so affected, by the sight of a woman's calves? It was ridiculous. And if he didn't stifle his reactions, stop giving her these signals, she'd be the one to do something about their attraction, he wouldn't be able to resist…and he'd end up hurting her.

"Hey, Mr. Barrington?"

He stopped and turned toward the sound of his name.

Standing by the Ferris-wheel-like apparatus that distributed assorted candies for packing, and wearing a white coat and a hairnet, a woman in her fifties smiled at him.

"Are you going to the company Christmas party Friday night?"

He took the few steps over to the candy wheel. "Actually, I didn't know there was a Christmas party."

"It's sort of employee-sponsored. We save the proceeds from the vending machines all year and in December we have enough to have a Christmas party."

She gave him the name of his own hotel as the venue for the party, but he hardly paid any attention. Paul McCoy couldn't even spare a few thousand dollars of the company's money to host a Christmas party for the people who worked for him all year? He was an abysmal general manager. Cullen intended to call his hotel that afternoon and pay for the party, and he also intended to have a few choice words with Paul.

"Sure. I'm going."

She grinned and waved a piece of candy at him. "Want a Peanut Butter Bite?"

The *no* that should have tripped off his tongue, tripped over itself. He hadn't had a piece of Barrington's Candies in at least ten years. The scents wafting through the factory combined with a vivid memory of the taste of sweet chocolate and smooth peanut butter, and somehow moved his feet closer to the packing cylinder.

"Actually, my favorite is caramel."

A younger woman stretched her gloved hand to the distributor and plucked off a piece of candy. "Here you go."

His mouth watering, Cullen took the chocolate-covered caramel she handed him. He popped it in his mouth and groaned.

"I'd forgotten how good this was."

The packing ladies giggled.

"Want another?"

"Maybe one for after lunch."

The first packer snagged a piece and set it in one of the little brown paper cups that lined the Barrington Candies boxes. "Here you go."

He smiled at her. "Thanks."

From her position in shipping at the back of the factory floor, Wendy watched Cullen, crossing her arms on her chest, pride swelling inside her. She wasn't entirely sure why he'd come onto the plant floor, but unlike his first trip to have her introduce him around, his demeanor was totally different. And he'd accepted candy from strangers.

She wanted to giggle, but didn't want to call attention to herself, which might shift the attention of the employees milling around her to Cullen. He was doing so well building the employees' confidence in him that she didn't want to ruin that.

She pulled in a breath and let it out slowly. He was such a good guy. Really good. The affection he had for Harry could be explained by Harry's charm. But the gracious way he'd agreed to ease the employees' worries about the company closing was all Cullen. He was a good-hearted person. A nice guy.

A nice guy who wouldn't even look at her now.

She watched him laughing with the packers, accepting the various pieces of candy they handed to him, until ultimately Jennie Ferguson gave him a box in which to store his goodies.

Wendy smiled at his silly behavior. He wasn't simply a good person; he was a fun person. Fun had been missing from her life for two long years and in a little over two weeks, Cullen had her toasting marshmallows, making cocoa from scratch, Christmas-shopping and kissing again. For the first time in months she'd actually thought about sex. Not because of a physical need but because of him. This gorgeous, sexy, sweet guy had her tiptoeing into uncharted territory. But she was a small-town girl with so little experience she constantly made mistakes with him.

Before anybody noticed her staring, she turned and began taking inventory of the items in the first aid kit in shipping and receiving.

Like Patty and Emma, she'd thought for sure he had come to her house last Thursday night to see her. But he couldn't even sit with her for two minutes after he'd read Harry's story. Now, he wouldn't look at her. She suspected he hadn't yet noticed that Emma and Patty had given her a makeover. And if he had, he'd probably realized she was dressing up for him and that was why he was keeping his distance.

This time she'd made a fool of herself without even opening her mouth.

She couldn't remember the last time she'd been so disappointed. So embarrassed. Seeing him laughing with the candy packers, her humiliation grew. She was the only person he seemed nervous around. Because of their damned attraction. Because he realized she wouldn't mind having an affair with him. Because she was now strutting around in skirts instead of slacks, wearing makeup…making a fool of herself!

He'd warned her off. But she couldn't take a hint and now she felt like an idiot.

* * *

With a box of assorted chocolates under his arm, Cullen glanced in the direction of shipping and receiving and didn't see Wendy.

He turned to his candy posse—which is what they'd told him to call them since they intended to make sure all his chocolate needs were met for the rest of his stay. "Anybody see where Wendy went?"

"She left through the side door," Annette said, pointing to the opposite end of the plant floor. "Probably on her way back to her office."

"Thanks."

He arrived in Wendy's office, smiling. After his encounter with the ladies in packing, he now understood that most of the people in this town were happy-go-lucky and generous with their time and attention. He didn't have to worry about Wendy. She wasn't falling for him. She was simply being nice to him because that's the way people in this town were.

Walking into her office, he displayed his box of chocolates. "Look what I got."

She didn't look up from her work. "That's nice."

"How can you say that's nice when you didn't even see what I have?"

"You have a box of chocolates."

"How do you know?"

"I saw you talking with the ladies in packing."

He thought about that for a second. She should be dancing for joy that he was doing as she asked, mingling, making himself seem normal, putting everybody's mind at ease that he and his father had no intention of closing the factory.

Yet she was angry. Why would she be angry that he talked with the packing ladies?

His eyes narrowed. Unless she was jealous?

A sweet pang of self-satisfaction danced in his belly. But he stopped it. That was ridiculous. First, she didn't seem like the kind of woman to be jealous. Second, he didn't want her to be jealous. Now that he understood what a bad idea it would be for them to have an affair, he wanted their relationship to be strictly professional.

"They're all very nice," he said softly, not quite sure what else to say.

She rose from her desk and walked with the safety binder to the filing cabinet. Sliding it into position with the other binders, she said, "Wasn't I the one who told you that?"

Her clipped tone made him sigh. "All right. What's wrong?"

"Nothing. I have work to do."

The sharp tone was a downgrade from the clipped tone. Whatever had her angry, it was getting worse. "Why are you angry?"

She spun to face him. "I'm *not* angry."

He took a step closer, set his candy on top of the filing cabinets and touched his index finger to the red spots flaring on her cheeks. "These say otherwise."

But as the words came out of his mouth, he realized she wasn't angry. She really was upset.

His index finger hovered above her soft cheeks, so it was a natural movement when his hand shifted to cup her jaw.

Her big green eyes blinked up at him and his pulse scrambled. He didn't take the time to evaluate the situation. Didn't give himself an opportunity to issue the three thousand warnings that were ringing like bells in his brain. The sweet syrupy feeling tightening his chest had him under its spell. It urged him to shift forward, just brush his lips across hers.

He did and wasn't sorry. Her taste was sweeter than a

thousand candies. Her soft mouth responded to his, naturally, honestly, sending another pang of need through him.

His hands fell to her waist, nudging her closer, and she melted in his arms.

But it was the way she melted with total trust that brought him to his senses. If they got involved, one way or another he would let her down. Even if things worked out the way she wanted and they fell in love, he knew love didn't last. His parents had sniped at each other for nearly forty years. When his mother had died, Cullen had actually struggled with the worry that his father had been relieved. Though he'd cried at her funeral, the next day he'd been off on his boat and soon he was out at parties with friends. In a week, it seemed that Cullen's mom had been forgotten by everybody but Cullen. There was no way he wanted that for himself. But more than that, there was no way he wanted that for Wendy.

He pulled away. She blinked up at him, her pretty green eyes bright. Her lips were glistening from his kiss.

He squeezed his eyes shut in misery. "I'm sorry. I shouldn't have done that. I don't want to give you the wrong impression. But most of all I don't want to hurt you."

CHAPTER TEN

STANDING by the filing cabinet with her lips still tingling from his kiss, Wendy watched Cullen race into his office. She noticed that he'd forgotten his candy but wasn't about to take it in to him. She was too stunned.

Not because he'd kissed her, but because he couldn't help himself. She hadn't made a fool of herself. He *liked* her, but he didn't want to hurt her.

She should feel that he was noble. She should even appreciate it. But part of her was annoyed. Maybe she and Cullen weren't meant to be together forever, but she needed this. She needed a few days or weeks with a man who truly couldn't resist her to make her feel strong and sexy again. He was leaving on Thursday of the following week. They didn't have enough time left together that she'd be paralyzed with pain when he left. So everything could be okay.

But she wouldn't be the one to pursue him. She refused to make a fool of herself. The embarrassment of the past few days had burned that lesson onto her brain.

She went back to work.

He went back to work.

And they didn't speak for the rest of the week, except when he needed something.

* * *

Friday at lunch the employee cafeteria was abuzz with the news that Cullen intended to attend the Christmas party. Sitting at her desk that afternoon, Wendy watched him, saddened that a wonderful opportunity was slipping through her fingers. Still, she couldn't be the one to make the first move. Especially not at the Christmas party. Too many people would be watching. Too much chance that her coworkers would see her embarrassment if he rejected her.

At five o'clock she dashed home, thinking she'd have to remind Mrs. Brennon that she was cooking dinner and babysitting that night. She found the plump older woman humming at the stove, stirring a pot of something that smelled like beef stew.

"You remembered!"

Mrs. Brennon nodded. "How could I forget dinner with such a handsome young man?"

Sitting at the table crayoning the pictures in a thick coloring book, Harry peered at Wendy over his glasses. "She means me."

Wendy walked over and hugged him. "Of course she means you."

"You scoot now," Mrs. Brennon said, waving her arms at Wendy. "You have a party to go to."

Wendy raced to her bedroom. The party began at seven. She needed an hour to dress. And there was the matter of the thirty-minute drive to the hotel. She didn't have a second to waste.

She quickly stripped and showered but spent far too long twisting her long hair into bouncy curls with the curling iron.

Realizing she had about ten minutes to get on the road or dinner would already be started, she raced to her closet. And stood staring at the dress she'd purchased the week before with Emma and Patty's guidance.

She pulled out the simple sleeveless red sheath and

examined it, wondering if she should wear it. They'd picked it knowing it would attract Cullen's attention. Short enough to reveal a bit of leg, but not embarrassingly short. Snug enough to cruise her curves but not too tight.

Would it be enough to attract his attention?

And if it wasn't, would she lose her patience and ask him to dance?

Could she risk another rejection?

Not entirely sure how to dress for this event, since he'd never attended a company Christmas party, Cullen decided on a plain black suit, a white shirt and a gold tie. That was about as festive as his wardrobe got when he was traveling. But when he stepped into the hotel's ballroom and saw that most of the men wore suits and ties, no tuxes, he relaxed.

He took a drink from a passing waiter and saw Wendy in the back of the room chatting with some people from shipping and receiving. The sleeveless red dress she wore was particularly flattering to her figure, and he let his gaze ripple from her head to her toes, pausing to take in the length of leg she exposed.

She'd never looked prettier or sexier, so he turned and walked in the other direction. Not because he wanted to avoid her, but because he needed to be careful around her. Especially in a room full of witnesses. If he lost control and kissed her again, that would be the talk of the factory on Monday morning. He still had almost a week to work here and the prospect of being teased or gossiped about didn't thrill him. Worse, Wendy had to work with these people forever. He wouldn't embarrass her.

The ladies in his candy posse corralled him and he accepted their invitation to sit at their table for dinner. Which was good. He'd avoided yet another opportunity to get too close to Wendy.

After dinner, the band shifted from dinner music to dance

music. Telling his posse that he needed to mingle, he excused himself and headed for the bar. He was stopped by so many people that the band finished their first set, took a break and began playing again before he actually made it.

He ordered a Scotch and suddenly found himself standing by Emma Watson and Patty Franks. "Good evening, Mr. Barrington."

"Good evening, ladies. Are you enjoying yourselves?"

"Yes. Thank you."

Patty blinked false eyelashes at him. "I haven't seen you dancing yet tonight."

"I sort of got waylaid."

"That's no excuse," she said with a laugh. Just when Cullen was absolutely positive she was about to ask him to dance, she shifted slightly. Wendy stood behind her. "I'm sure Wendy would love to dance."

From the way Wendy's eyes widened with fear, Cullen not only knew her friends had surprised her, but also that dancing with him was probably the absolute last thing she wanted to do. But because she was afraid, not eager, he knew they would be safe together. Saying no or making a fuss would only call more attention to them than if they simply complied and danced to one song.

He held out his hand. "Would you care to dance?"

She swallowed and looked at her two friends who were smirking with victory before she placed her hand in his. "Sure."

He led her out to the crowded floor just as the band stopped playing a hopping fast tune and began playing something slow. He caught her gaze. "If you'd rather not—"

She grimaced. "They'll just keep hounding us until we dance, so we might as well get this over with."

Taking her into his arms, he said, "Just what every guy wants to hear."

She laughed. "Sorry."

She fit so perfectly and felt so good that Cullen nearly groaned. Luckily, Wendy tilted her head back and said, "You're a big hit."

He laughed. "Thanks to my love of candy and my candy posse."

"Rumor has it you paid for the party."

He shrugged. "It's the least my father and I can do."

"Well, that gesture's gone a long way to improve employee morale."

"Nobody thinks the plant is closing anymore?"

She shook her head and gave him another sweet smile. "No. Thank you."

"These people should be thanking you."

She shrugged. "Not really. I was just being a good assistant. Filling you in on things you should know."

He pulled back, caught her gaze. "You really can't be that good."

Her pretty face scrunched in confusion, as her eyes lit with laughter. "What do you mean *good*?"

She truly didn't get it. She didn't understand that she was beautiful, sexy and intriguing enough to draw a jaded man like himself to her and then sweet enough to make him almost believe in Christmas wishes.

"You're very nice to people."

"No. I simply treat people the way I want to be treated."

He groaned. "Stop."

Wendy tilted her face up to him. "Stop what?"

"Stop being so nice."

She laughed. "I'm not always nice."

The look in her eyes told him exactly what she was thinking. He was the person she didn't want to be "nice" with and he could almost envision the naughtiness she hinted at. The temptation to kiss her was nearly overwhelming. But she wasn't one of the pampered socialites he typically dated. He couldn't be flippant with her—tease her, take her home and make love until dawn—then go back to being her boss on Monday morning.

Still, he might not be able to make love with her or even kiss her, but he couldn't stop himself from dipping her on the dance floor, and was rewarded with a giggle.

"Stop that," she admonished, but her words poured out through a laugh. "This isn't *Dancing with the Stars*."

He laughed, too, and whirled her around. He might not ever get to sleep with her, but why couldn't they spend this last hour of the evening simply enjoying each other's company? If there was one thing he'd learned about her in the three weeks they'd been together, it was that he was always himself, always had fun in her company.

The night suddenly felt young and full of possibilities. No one had ever made him as happy as Wendy did.

The thought that she'd become so special to him caused him to ease back a bit, once again not wanting to start something he couldn't finish. But he suddenly realized that this might be the one and only time in his life when he'd allow himself to feel this close to someone. In Miami, he'd go back to dating spoiled socialites. His life would be all about hiding who he was, what he cared about, so no one could get too close. He *wanted* this. He wanted this hour of simply having fun. He wanted it enough to convince himself that if he returned to his typical boss self on Monday morning, the way Cinderella's coach returned to being a pumpkin at the stroke of midnight, she'd take this night for what it was—one fabulous hour filled with joy—but she'd also realize anything more wasn't to be.

Wendy felt the shift in him. Rather than being stiff and polite, he relaxed. His arms wrapped around her possessively. His cheek pressed against her temple. She could match the soft puff of breath near her ear to the gentle rhythm of his chest rising and falling against hers.

At first she stiffened. If she misinterpreted this, she would make a huge fool of herself. But he tightened his hold and pulled her closer. He smelled so damned good that she weakened. Her bones seemed to melt and she cuddled closer.

When the song ended, she pulled back, out of his embrace, but he caught her hand and stopped her. "There's no reason to leave the dance floor."

Her heart kicked into overdrive. "You want to dance again?"

The band began playing another slow tune and he smiled. "Yes."

She swallowed. "Okay."

By the end of the second dance, Wendy felt gooey inside. They didn't have to speak for her to feel them growing closer.

The band started a fast song and Cullen grabbed her hand. Thinking he was leading them to the bar, she was surprised when he walked out of the ballroom and into the brightly lit lobby. Using his room key card, he opened a door that led to a dark and silent atrium.

She stepped inside. "Wow."

"There's a pool just beyond that garden." He pointed to a large circle of tropical plants beneath a skylight that revealed a million stars twinkling in a sea of black sky. "It's locked to anyone but hotel guests."

Her eyes widening, she spun to face him. "We're not—You're not thinking of swimming—"

He laughed. "No. I don't want to swim. I just wanted some privacy."

She stepped away. "Oh."

"You don't have to be afraid."

"I'm not afraid." She walked over to the circle of plants that hid the pool from view of anyone in the lobby. "I always wondered how they got these to grow here."

"Climate control and sunlamps."

She tilted her head. "That makes sense."

"Yep."

This time his answer came from directly behind her. His hands fell to her shoulders and he turned her around. "I also didn't bring you here to talk about the plants."

"What do you want to talk about?"

He shrugged. "I don't know. Your plans for the future."

Her heart stuttered. Her pulse scrambled. She nearly asked him why he'd be concerned about her future, but didn't want to look needy. Silly. There were only two reasons he would ask. One, he was worried about her. Or, two, he wanted to be part of her future and wondered if he fit into it.

She liked number two better.

Considering what she'd say, she caught his gaze. "I… um…have to take care of Harry. That's my number-one priority."

"Anything else?"

Suddenly feeling flirtatious, she stepped away. "I want lots of things."

He followed her, but she continued to stay just out of his reach. "Like what?"

"Well, I'd like to fix up my house."

He grimaced. "You want to stay there?"

She turned to face him, let him catch up to her. "Yes. It's a beautiful house."

"No. It's a solid house. A sturdy house. With a little work it might be beautiful."

"All the more reason to keep it. It's dependable. I can make that house a home for me and Harry."

Holding her gaze, Cullen tilted his head. "Yes. I think you can."

Then he kissed her and she didn't hesitate to wrap her arms around him. He was staying at this hotel. In one short elevator ride they could be behind closed doors with no worries that anyone else in the hotel with a room key could pop in on them. Then she'd have him all to herself.

Just the thought made her heart skip a beat and filled her with fear. She didn't just want a fling. Cullen was perfect. Wonderful. She'd fallen in love with him. And it appeared he was falling in love with her, too.

He pulled away slowly. His voice was a mere whisper when he said, "Let's get out of here."

She nodded. Cullen caught her hand and led her into the lobby, but instead of heading for the elevator he walked her to the coat room. At first she was confused, then she remembered that the coat room would be locked by the time she came downstairs, and she'd either have to ask at the front desk to be let in to get her coat, or slink home without one.

But instead of slinging her coat over his arm, he helped her into it.

"Party's about over," he said, taking her hand and leading her to the hotel entrance. "This way, we'll miss the crowd."

They walked in silence across the cold parking lot. A

million thoughts swirled through her head. But she said nothing because she had no idea what he was doing.

When they reached her little blue vehicle, she said, "Why did you walk me to my car?"

He caught her hand, lifted it to his lips. "Come on, Cinderella. You didn't really think I was going to miss this opportunity, did you?"

He said the words as he bent to kiss her and Wendy's head spun. With one coaxing swipe from the tip of his tongue she opened her mouth to him. He drew her so close that their bodies melded together and she cursed her black wool winter coat. The kiss went on and on, warming her blood, making her forget her own name, and suddenly he pulled away. Stepped away.

"Good night."

Her breath puffed out in confusion, until she realized he probably knew she had to get home to Harry. She smiled. For once his noble gesture really was a noble gesture. She also couldn't really argue with him. As much as she'd love to walk back into that hotel with him and finish what they'd started, he was right. Harry needed her. Plus, they had at least the week he was in Barrington to follow up on this.

Maybe more.

She couldn't stop her heart from wishing that maybe, just maybe, what had started this Christmas could extend throughout the year.

But that was a wish for another night. Tonight, she simply wanted to bask in the joy that he really did like her, as much as she liked him.

And they had another week.

* * *

Cullen flew home to Miami on Saturday morning.

"Are you home for good?" his dad asked, not looking up from his newspaper.

Cullen carefully set his briefcase on the counter. "I have a few more days to finish out, Dad."

"Uh-huh." His dad's voice dripped with skepticism as he folded the paper and tossed it aside. "We got a call from Paul McCoy last night. He quit."

All the breath rushed out of Cullen's lungs. "What?"

"He lied to us. He wasn't on an extended vacation. He had bypass surgery. Seems that the whole process left him feeling life's too short to work it away and he's choosing not to come back."

Cullen fell to one of the breakfast-nook chairs. His immediate reaction was that he could run the factory, but he stopped it. Even the *suggestion* would infuriate his dad—which was probably why his father was behaving so oddly. Plus, he'd be giving up the life he'd created here in Miami. The life he loved.

The lust still racing through his blood from a few simple kisses the night before reminded him that maybe he could love another life. As clear as a bell, he could see himself marrying Wendy, fixing up the old monstrosity that had been in his family for generations before Wendy had bought it, and raising Harry.

A bubble of joy formed in his chest. As if the entirety of his life had been leading him to this moment. This decision.

His father's voice brought him back to reality. "I already called an employment agency. They're setting up interviews for Sunday afternoon and Monday morning at your hotel."

"That was fast."

"I offered the recruiter a bonus if we could have a firm yes from someone before Christmas."

"That's not much time."

"It's a week. The economy is down. Lots of people are looking for work. Some people will consider a shot at this job their Christmas miracle."

And suddenly Cullen saw the truth. "You don't want to risk me staying."

Donald Barrington pulled in a breath. "I'm seeing some signs I don't like, Cullen." He reached for his coffee. "Don't get me wrong. I'm not so prejudiced that I don't know that there are some nice people in Barrington. Good people. But the truth is that that factory sucks Barringtons into a black hole that never lets them out. Look what happened to your mother."

"I'm not my mother."

"No. You're not. You're more like me. You'll find a woman that you really love and who you think loves you, and *she'll* tie you to the factory. You might not think so at first. You'll be so far in lust with her you'll think you'll be happy forever. But one day you'll get bored with the factory and you'll suggest you hire a replacement so you can come back to the life you love here, and she'll say no. She doesn't want to leave her friends. And you'll start noticing she cares more about her coworkers than she cares about you and you'll wonder if she ever cared about you at all."

Cullen licked his suddenly dry lips. He never realized how much his relationship with Wendy was like his parents' relationship. "I can always get a divorce."

"And never see your child? That's how she'll hold you, you know. She'll convince you to have a child or two and then tell you that if you move you'll never see your child again."

He swallowed. "Was that what mom threatened?"

"Yes. Not because she intended to ask a judge to preclude me from seeing you, but because she knew I'd be moving thousands of miles away. She didn't have to threaten me. School would keep you in Barrington. And I'd see you in the summers. If I was lucky."

"You stayed married for me?"

"Yes."

Cullen's stomach sank and his world spun. So many things that hadn't made sense suddenly did. His father had stayed for *him*. He might not have coached Little League or even spent inordinate amounts of time with him, but he'd kept the bond so when they finally could move away they'd have time together. As much as Cullen wanted.

And now Cullen was considering abandoning him. For a woman he barely knew. A woman who'd already worked some kind of magic on him to get him involved with the employees and to like them.

Donald Barrington rose to get another cup of coffee, bringing Cullen out of his reverie. "I was going to do the interviews but if you want to—"

"I'll do it."

He didn't believe Wendy had faked her feelings for him, but they didn't know each other well enough for him to say they wouldn't end up like his parents.

He wouldn't take the job of running Barrington Candies, but he did owe her an explanation. He simply didn't know how or when he'd make it.

CHAPTER ELEVEN

CULLEN arrived so late on Monday afternoon that Wendy would have missed him if she hadn't been a few minutes behind in leaving for the day.

Just the sight of him made her heart sing. "Hey."

His voice was soft and solemn, when he said, "Hey."

"What's wrong?"

"Nothing." He paused. "I'm just tired."

"After traveling from Miami, I suppose you have a right to be tired."

"Yeah." He pulled in a breath. "You go on home. I have everything I need."

"You're working?"

"Yeah."

"Okay," she said, understanding, but unable to stop the swell of disappointment that poured through her. Now that the weekend was gone, they had three days—three short days—to see if they could have something before he returned to Miami— and he'd scheduled himself to work one of those nights.

It didn't make sense, unless she'd misinterpreted everything on Friday night. After all, they'd only shared a few mind-blowing kisses. A guy like Cullen Barrington probably kissed hundreds of girls. What had been magic for her might have been normal for him.

"I'll see you in the morning," she said lightly, leaving the office with her dignity intact. But her heart hurt. She didn't know if he was really busy or backing off, and she was too inexperienced to figure it out. Worse, the situation was too fragile to call Patty for an interpretation.

"Hey, Wendy. Can I ask you a question?"

Wendy turned from the dishwasher with a smile for Harry. She didn't have any idea what was going on with Cullen, but she did know she couldn't let it affect Harry. "Sure."

"Can we go see Santa tonight?"

She'd totally forgotten about the trip to see Santa. The news of Harry's father's death had completely wiped it off her radar screen, and time was running out. With only four days until Christmas, if they didn't go see Santa soon, their chance would be gone.

Miserable or not, she needed to take him to see Santa. Plus, getting out of the house might get her mind off Cullen.

"Sure. Why not?"

"Yes!" Harry said, doing a victory hand pump.

"Go upstairs and change your shirt and comb your hair, while I finish the dishes."

"Okay."

Harry scrambled off his chair and raced into the hall and up the stairs. He passed his room and stopped in front of Wendy's. With a quick look behind him to make sure she hadn't followed him, he darted inside and rifled in his jeans pocket for the scrap of paper he'd torn out of his notebook.

As Harry picked up the phone, Creamsicle ambled into

Wendy's bedroom. He plopped beside Harry's feet, his bell chiming.

"There's no point in ringing that bell if they're never together," Harry said as he punched the number for Cullen's cell phone into the phone on Wendy's bedside table. Cullen answered on the second ring.

"Hey, Cullen!"

"Hey, kid. What's up? There's nothing wrong, is there?"

"No. Wendy's taking me to see Santa tonight."

Cullen settled more comfortably against the headboard of his hotel-room bed. He'd just finished his final interview. After talking with fifteen various and sundry potential plant managers, he'd decided that Tom Ross had all the qualifications they were looking for. Cullen had not only given him a tour of the plant, Tom had also accepted the job. He had to work out a two-week notice, but after the rush for Christmas, Barrington Candies closed for two weeks for the holiday, so Tom would be available the first day Barrington Candies went back to work.

His head spinning from the hectic pace of the past two days, Cullen could use a few minutes of mindless conversation with the little boy he'd miss more than he'd ever imagined.

"That's great. Are you going to sit on his lap?"

"Yep. And somebody will take a picture of me."

"It's usually an elf."

Harry laughed. Cullen smiled. The kid was too damned cute.

"So if you want to, you could come with us."

His chest tightened. He'd pay good money for a little more time with Wendy, real time, private time, but he'd started the process of distancing himself from her that afternoon. It wasn't a good idea to give her the wrong impression. He knew firsthand what happened to a marriage when love left. He didn't want what his parents had. A miserable shell of a relationship where they argued more than they talked.

And he was already half in love with Harry. That's why it was so easy for him to understand why his dad had stayed, why he hadn't divorced his mother and moved on. He didn't want to lose touch with his son. He and his dad might not have had a perfect relationship, but his dad had been there every night. When Cullen became a man and his father and mother had moved to Miami to be with him, they'd had a relationship to build on. Cullen could see himself doing the same thing for Harry—staying with Wendy even after the love died, if only to keep enough contact with Harry that they could have a relationship when Harry became an adult.

It was better to stop things between him and Wendy before he got to the point where he fell in love, made some bad choices and ended up hurting everybody.

"I don't think so—"

"Really?" Harry's happy voice shifted to unhappy without missing a beat. "You should see Santa, too."

"Santa stopped bringing me presents years ago."

"But if you're there when I'm talking to him, you'll hear what I want when I tell him."

Cullen stifled a laugh. The little dickens was making sure that he got everything he wanted for Christmas. "What if I want to surprise you with my gift?"

"What if you're so old you don't know what to get me?"

This time Cullen did laugh. The kid had a point. Wendy had approved the fire truck he'd already purchased, but one fire truck was hardly a good gift for a kid who'd had such a rough year. He wanted to shower him with presents, but he knew they should be gifts Harry wanted. Plus, if he continued to be impersonal and businesslike with Wendy tonight, he could drive home his point about their relationship. Friday night had been fun, but it was over. If she asked why he was distant, he could actually tell her that without worrying that one of her coworkers might overhear. He could make a clean, honest break with her.

He might also get a chance to tell her about the new plant manager. He didn't want her to walk in the Monday after Christmas vacation and discover she had a new boss—a boss Cullen had hired—yet Cullen hadn't told her.

He owed her that much.

"All right. What time are you going?"

"We're leaving as soon as I get a clean shirt on."

"Then go get a clean shirt on."

Walking to the closet to retrieve his jacket, Cullen was hit by a bolt of uncertainty. He'd never been around Wendy when he didn't melt a little. She made him laugh. She made him happy.

He squeezed his eyes shut. At one point his mother had made his dad happy. She'd made him laugh. And he'd made all the wrong choices in his life, mostly to ensure he didn't lose his only child.

And Cullen had had a front-row seat not only to his dad's misery, but to his mom's. So, no. There was no worry he'd make the same mistakes his father had.

The mall was alive with Christmas music and happy people. Holding Harry's hand, Wendy guided him toward the roped-off area where Santa sat. Two elves guarded the break in the ropes that served as an entry. A rotund man wearing a red suit and fake white hair and beard sat on a gold throne. Two more elves stood by his side. One held candy canes. The other held a bag of toys. Previews of things to come, Wendy suspected.

She expected Harry to race up to the display, instead he held back.

"What's wrong?"

He blinked up at her then pushed his glasses up his nose. "There are no bells here."

She laughed. Sometimes his mind worked in the weirdest ways. "Bells?"

"You know. Silver bells like the song."

"Oh! Well, silver bells are only a part of Christmas. Just like you don't see Santa everywhere or elves in every decoration or display, silver bells aren't mandatory."

Even as she said the last, she saw Cullen striding toward them from the far end of the mall. At the same time, a man dressed in a reindeer suit stepped over the green velvet ropes into the Santa display. The collar of sleigh bells that he wore jingled merrily.

Harry grinned up at her. "Never mind. Everything's okay now." He turned to Cullen as he approached. "Hey, Cullen!"

"Hey, Harry!" He smiled at Wendy. "Wendy."

Her heart skipped a beat. He was here! Maybe she'd misinterpreted what happened between them that afternoon?

She stopped herself. She was *not* going to be "that" girl. The one who embarrassed herself over a man who really didn't want her. He'd hardly spoken to her that afternoon. She'd felt a distance between them. Something had been wrong. She couldn't assume he was here to see her. It was probably a coincidence they were at the mall at the same time.

"Hello, Cullen."

"I hope you don't mind, but Harry invited me."

She looked down at the little boy. "You did?"

He nodded. "He needs to know what I want for Christmas, too."

She was glad Cullen had made a special effort for Harry, but that only made his dismissal of her more obvious. Why had he romanced her on Friday night if he didn't want her? No. That wasn't the question. The real question was why had she fallen for everything he'd said Friday night? He was a playboy. She knew it. She should have protected herself. But she hadn't, and now her heart ached.

But tonight wasn't about her. She had a son to raise, and tonight he wanted to see Santa. She'd think about this, berate herself, feel bad tomorrow.

"All right. Let's go." She pointed at the short line by the Santa display. "It must have been a smart idea to come on a weeknight because there's no line."

Harry looked at Cullen. "You can't hear from back here. You have to come with us."

"Sure. Lead the way."

Harry danced over to the booth behind the green velvet ropes, Wendy and Cullen on his heels. The reindeer at the cash register told Wendy the price of the picture and she reached for her purse but before she could even open it, Cullen handed the man enough money for two pictures.

Her heart twisted in her chest at the thought that he loved Harry enough that he wanted a picture of him to remember him by. But that only meant she'd have to be doubly careful that his kindness to Harry didn't make her starry-eyed again.

Handing Cullen's change to him, the reindeer leaned forward and his collar of sleigh bells jingled merrily. Harry squeezed Wendy's hand.

She laughed. "You really like bells, don't you?"

He nodded solemnly. "I love bells."

A tall thin blonde in a red velvet outfit that looked more like a French maid's uniform than an elf suit walked over and caught Cullen's arm, walking him to Santa. Behind them, Wendy experienced a twist of jealousy. *That* was the kind of woman a man like Cullen Barrington belonged with. Sexy and not afraid to flaunt it. Not a crazed assistant whose fondest wish was to create a real home for a six-year-old boy who'd lost his mom, who wouldn't wear a French maid's outfit on a lost bet and who preferred hot cocoa to hot toddies.

She had to remember that. She had to accept the reality that they might be attracted, but they weren't a match made in heaven, and she had to stop wishing for things that couldn't come true.

When they reached Santa's throne, the old man called, "Come on up, little boy, and my photographer, Frenchie, will take your picture."

Harry scrambled up the steps to Santa's throne. Frenchie ambled to the camera sitting on the tripod about six feet away.

"That's certainly an apt nickname," Wendy murmured.

Cullen faced her. "Excuse me?"

She cleared her throat. "Never mind."

"No. You said something. What was it?"

"I said her nickname is appropriate."

Cullen studied her for a second then laughed and shook his head. "Women. Dress another woman up in something scanty and you all turn into the preacher's wife."

She sniffed the air. "This is a child's display."

"Yeah, but I'm guessing old Frenchie brings in her fair share of single dads and this is a money-making enterprise. Santa's not here out of the goodness of his heart."

She couldn't argue with that, but she didn't like the hot string of jealousy threading through her. So she kept her mouth shut. The song being piped through the intercom system ended and was quickly replaced by "Silver Bells."

Harry beamed. Wendy gave him a thumbs-up signal.

"What was that for?"

"He likes bells."

Cullen laughed. "I've noticed that, too."

"It's probably a normal kid fixation."

He nodded. "When I was six I loved the garbage truck."

"Really? I loved the mail truck."

"You liked getting surprises."

"That's better than wanting to see the trash leave."

Cullen laughed again. "Though I can't deny that I loved watching the trash disappear, I have to confess I was more in love with the hydraulics."

"Really?"

"Why are you so surprised?"

They turned simultaneously; their gazes caught and clung. Memories of the Christmas party danced like sugar-plum fairies through her head. Especially the goodnight kiss. She felt the warmth of it to her toes. Remembered every delicious sensation and the way her softness melted into his strength. And knew from the way his eyes heated that he was remembering it, too.

"I guess I shouldn't be surprised."

The words came out as a soft whisper as she fought the urge to step closer, to satisfy her curiosity about him with a hundred personal questions, to tell him all her secrets and dreams.

"No. You shouldn't." His words were soft, too, filled with an emotion she couldn't identify, though she could see the struggle taking place inside him from the way his eyes flickered. He liked her, maybe even wanted to love her, but something stopped him.

A burst of desperation overwhelmed her. She *loved* him. She loved everything about him. And he absolutely wanted to love her. But something held him back. Still, every time they had a personal conversation a chip of his resolve fell away. If they had enough time together, he wouldn't be able to resist the pull. He'd fall in love, too. But they didn't have time. He would be leaving in a day or two.

Holding his gaze, she drew in a soft breath and did something she hadn't done in at least a decade. She made a wish. Not that he'd love her, but that he'd stay. Not forever, but long enough for them to give what they felt a chance. She didn't want to live her life wondering if her chance at true love had gone because he didn't have enough time to realize he loved her. She wanted to know if he was the one…or if he wasn't.

Then if he loved her, *they* could go to Miami. They could move to the moon. She didn't care. But he'd be going alone if they didn't have at least another month together, maybe two.

She wished it. She opened her heart to the universe and wished, just as the reindeer stepped out of the booth, his sleigh bells jingling.

"Cullen Barrington?"

The man tapping on Cullen's shoulder caused Cullen to break eye contact with Wendy and he was glad. He could feel himself weakening again, longing for something that couldn't be.

"Skinny?"

Richard "Skinny" Pedrosky laughed. Now six feet tall, with a body obviously built by hours in a gym, sandy-brown hair and blue eyes, Rich was no longer the ugly-duckling runt he'd been in high school.

"Most people call me Rich now."

"I'll be damned!" Cullen said, extending his hand for shaking. "How are you?"

"I'm fine." Without missing a beat, he added, "Who's your friend?"

"Oh, this is Wendy Winston. She's my admin while I'm in Barrington running the factory."

Leaning forward to take the hand Rich extended, Wendy smiled. "It's nice to meet you."

"Please tell me you aren't here because you have a child visiting Santa."

"I do."

"Damn," Rich said. "All the good ones are taken."

Wendy laughed. "I'm not taken. I was awarded custody of my neighbor's son when she passed a few weeks ago."

Rich said, "Oh, I'm sorry." But the gleam in his eyes didn't match his words.

Something hot and angry bubbled up in Cullen's stomach. He told himself to settle down, told himself it shouldn't matter that another man was interested in Wendy. It didn't quite work, but Rich shifted his gaze from Wendy back to Cullen, forcing him to school his expression into one of complete apathy, as if it made no difference one way or another if Rich flirted with Wendy.

"I hear your plant manager resigned."

"What?" Wendy gasped her reaction before Cullen could reply.

He turned to her. It wasn't how he'd planned to tell her, but he'd wanted an opportunity and this was it.

"Mr. McCoy was close to retirement age. He actually took vacation to have bypass surgery."

Her eyes widened in shock.

"He's fine, but he decided life was too short to spend it working and he won't be back."

"Wow."

He watched her delicate features shift and change as she processed that. Finally she said, "I guess I'm not really surprised. His taking time off in December was odd." She raised her gaze to meet his, her eyes so full of hope that Cullen froze.

"Do you have a replacement?"

The question hung in the air between them. Their gazes held. The world around them shifted to slow motion, and for Cullen all sound stopped. He knew what she was thinking. He could take the job. They could explore what they felt for each other. He could help raise Harry.

He swallowed. Even though he'd already counted himself out, even though he knew he'd someday hurt Wendy if he pursued this attraction, it was suddenly all so tempting.

Once again, Rich interrupted. "Yeah, Cullen," he said, shifting just slightly to stand beside Wendy, giving Cullen an instant vision of what they'd look like as a couple. "That's actually why I'm glad to have run into you. I'd like to be considered."

Cullen's world spun. He felt like a sorcerer overwhelmed by a mystic vision of the future. They looked good together, perfect. Even as half of him screamed in protest, the logical half really could see their future. *Wendy's* future. Security with somebody stable. A real father for Harry, instead of a man who couldn't even be sure he was capable of staying for the long haul. If he gave in to everything he felt for her and they failed, she'd miss her opportunity with someone like Rich, someone who was right for her.

The reindeer walked over and tapped Cullen on the shoulder, the bells of his collar jingling pleasantly. "Hey, your kid wants you to look at him."

Red-faced, Cullen quickly turned and waved at Harry. But Harry wasn't upset, as Cullen had thought he would be. Instead he grinned. "I'm telling Santa what I want. You should be closer."

Rich stepped back. "I didn't mean to interrupt. Is there somewhere I can send a résumé?"

Cullen nearly told him not to bother, he'd hired a replacement already, and then he remembered the vision. Wendy would be happy with Rich, and a man who truly liked her would want to see her happy. Though he'd given the job to someone else, if that candidate didn't work out, Rich might.

"Send it to my hotel."

As Rich nodded and turned away, Wendy realized Cullen had answered her question about having a replacement by telling Rich to submit his résumé. If he had a replacement, he wouldn't need more résumés. Cullen would be staying long enough to do interviews and make the decision.

Her wish had come true.

He might not be staying forever, but they had time.

She nearly lost her breath with joy, but Santa's laughter brought her back to reality.

"Ho. Ho. Ho. Little boy! Before we get to presents, I have to ask you if you were naughty or nice this year. Do you really want your parents to hear your answer?"

"Oh, they're not my parents. And they know I've been nice," Harry said as Cullen and Wendy approached the platform of Santa's throne. He leaned closer. "My mom was sick. I wasn't allowed to do a lot so Wendy and Cullen are making it up to me."

Santa said, "Oh, well, I'm sorry to hear that." He caught Cullen's gaze, then Wendy's. "I'm sure these two nice people won't let you down."

"We won't," Wendy said, stepping close enough to pat Harry's knee. "Go ahead. Tell Santa what you'd like for Christmas."

Harry gave a long rambling list. Wendy surreptitiously glanced over at Cullen and could see from the expression on his face that he was memorizing it. Her heart swelled. He was such a good guy. Now that he was staying, she could allow herself the feelings she had for him, and maybe even start showing him how she felt.

Harry finished his list. Santa laughed and winked at Cullen and Wendy. "There you go, little boy. Don't forget to be good these last few days before Christmas!"

"Oh, I will!" Harry said, scurrying off the man's lap and over to Wendy and Cullen. "Did you catch all that?"

"I did," Cullen said, scooping Harry off the floor and over his shoulder.

Frenchie quickly printed and framed Harry's pictures in simple cardboard frames and handed them to Wendy.

"But you know you're not getting everything, right?"

"That's why I have such a long list."

Wendy wasn't exactly sure of Harry's rationale, but it made her laugh. How could she not feel giddy? She'd have lots of time with Cullen. At least long enough for him to find a replacement for Mr. McCoy. Now all she had to do was use that time. Not waste it. Get herself some better clothes, some perfume, and take every opportunity to show Cullen they belonged together.

And considering that they were already together, this was one of those moments she wasn't going to let pass.

"How about a pretzel?"

From his perch on Cullen's shoulders, Harry said, "I want cinnamon."

Cullen hesitated for a second, and then said, "I'm a simple cheese and mustard guy."

"Me, too," Wendy agreed.

He slid Harry to the floor. "You two get a bench. I'll get the pretzels."

The number of mall shoppers seemed to have doubled while Harry sat on Santa's lap. Wendy scanned the densely populated concourse, looking for an empty bench and found one. Catching Cullen's gaze, she motioned to the bench, he nodded, and she and Harry trotted off to the seat.

After a short wait in line, Cullen walked over with the pretzels. "Cinnamon and sugar for you." He handed a pretzel and napkin to Harry. "And cheese and mustard for you."

Wendy took the pretzel he handed her. "Thanks."

Without meeting her gaze, he said, "You're welcome."

He sat on the far end of the bench, with Harry between them. But, again, Wendy wasn't dismayed. Something hummed between them. With the time they now had together, everything would fall into place. She simply had to have faith.

Wendy took a bite of her pretzel, chewed and swallowed. Smiling over Harry's head at Cullen, she said, "This is good. Thanks."

Harry grinned up at Cullen. "Yeah. Thanks."

A tall girl with purple hair, wearing black and white striped tights, an oversize sweatshirt and a ring of sleigh bells around each ankle walked by. The cacophony of tinkling bells caused Harry to look from Wendy to Cullen and burst into another round of giggles.

Cullen peered at Wendy over Harry's head. Wendy shrugged. "What's with you and bells?"

Harry glanced from Wendy to Cullen and back at Wendy again. "I use them to make wishes."

"Wishes?" Cullen asked, his brow wrinkling in confusion. "What kind of wishes?"

"When my mom was sick, I would wish every day that she would get better, but she never did."

Wendy's heart splintered in her chest. "Oh, Harry," she

said, tapping his forearm to get his attention. "That wasn't your fault. Not all wishes can come true."

"I know," he said solemnly. "But this time I have a plan." He looked from Wendy to Cullen. "Every time I hear a bell ring I make a wish."

Cullen chuckled. "That's very cute, but you can't put too much stock in wishes."

"But you can't stop wishing altogether!" Wendy disagreed. She believed in wishes. She had to. *Hers* had just come true. She couldn't let Cullen's opinion steal Harry's natural sense of wonder. Particularly in light of his already difficult life.

"Some wishes are wonderful and prove that sometimes life can be magical. What did you wish for?"

Harry peered at her over his glasses. "I can't tell you."

"Sure you can," Wendy said, clasping his hand reassuringly. "Because, just like with telling Santa what you want for Christmas, sometimes wishes come true because other people in your life make them happen for you. But that means the people in your life have to know what you want."

Cullen frowned thoughtfully. "You know what, Harry? She has a point. Shared wishes have a better chance of coming true because people who love you will try to make them come true."

Harry blinked up at them. "Really?"

They nodded.

"You want me to tell you?"

"Yes."

"Okay." He pulled in a breath. "Every time I hear a bell ring I wish for you two to get married and be my mom and dad."

Wendy's heart just about burst in her chest. "Oh, Harry!"

Cullen shifted his feet uncomfortably.

Harry looked from her to Cullen. "So, I told you. Can you make it come true?"

"Look, little guy—" Cullen paused to pull in a difficult breath. "The other reason it's good to tell adults your wishes is so that they can help you not get your hopes up. Wendy and I aren't going to get married. I'm leaving in a couple of days."

"But you said—"

"We said that sometimes grown-ups can help your wish come true. Not always." Wendy swallowed, and her eyes filled with tears. He wasn't staying? He *had* to stay. He had to find a replacement. How could he be leaving?

Cullen caught Harry's attention. "Wendy and I are friends. But that's it. I live in Miami. Very far away. I'm going home the day before Christmas Eve. There isn't enough time for Wendy and me to get to know each other enough to fall in love."

Their eyes met over Harry's head and to her embarrassment, Wendy found herself blinking back tears. Tears for Harry. Tears for herself. She was so stupid. She knew all this. Plus he'd never said he was staying to find Paul McCoy's replacement. She'd assumed he would be, because it was the answer to her foolish wish.

"That's true, Harry," she said softly.

The child gaped at her. "But you didn't know me long, and you took me and you said you love me."

"I do!"

"Then why don't you love Cullen?"

She scrambled to think of an answer but none came. She *did* love Cullen. That was why this hurt so much.

She swallowed.

Cullen balled up his pretzel paper and napkin and handed them to Harry. "Would you take this to the trash for me?"

Harry blinked, said, "Okay," and scampered off the bench.

Cullen grabbed her hand. "Wendy, I'm so sorry."

"For what? Both of us encouraged Harry to tell us his wish—"

"Not about the wish. He's a kid. He'll bounce back from this. It's you I want to apologize to."

"For what?" she asked again, fighting the stupid tears that kept filling her eyes. "All along I realized you didn't want me. We've been attracted from the second I fell on the ice into your arms." She shrugged. "We both knew it. But we also both knew it wouldn't come to anything."

He studied her face for several seconds. She knew her eyes brimmed with tears and her nose was probably red from holding back her sniffles. He had to see.

Hoping to save a bit of her pride, she switched the focus of the conversation. "I'm just a bit confused and surprised since I thought you'd be staying long enough to replace Mr. McCoy."

"I've already done the interviews." He pulled in a breath. "That's why I was busy tonight. I gave Mr. McCoy's replacement a tour of the plant."

"Then why take your friend's résumé?"

"In case Tom doesn't work out."

"Oh. Great." She struggled to take it all in and accept it, but it was too much. He'd probably known for days, maybe weeks that Mr. McCoy wasn't coming back, but he hadn't told her. If she needed any more proof that she had meant nothing to him, he'd just provided it. "That's good then."

He shifted uncomfortably on his seat and Wendy wished the ground would swallow her up. Finally, rubbing his hand across the back of his neck, he said, "Look, I'm sorry."

"You don't owe me an apology."

"I think I do. Not because I'm leaving, but because I've been trying like hell to stay away from you and sometimes I couldn't and I know I gave you the wrong impression."

"It's fine. I'm a big girl. I'll be okay."

"You're such a wonderful person, you deserve better than me. I'm ridiculously scarred. My parents had a really crappy marriage and—"

"I know. You told me. They wanted two different things. Your dad stayed because he loved your mom. But neither of them was ever happy."

"No, my dad stayed because he loved *me*. Had he divorced her and moved away he would have lost me. But both of them were miserable." He shook his head sadly. "I see it happen all the time. Friends so in love they can hardly wait to get married are divorced two years later." He caught her gaze. "I won't do that to you."

"I wouldn't do that to you."

He frowned. "You wouldn't what? Divorce me?"

"No." She caught his gaze. "I wouldn't fall out of love."

Her answer seemed to shock him, which seemed to make him angry. "How do you know?"

"I'd commit."

"My parents committed!"

"Not really. I think your parents fell in lust and when the lust was gone they were stuck. If they had really loved each other, they wouldn't have hurt each other. If you really loved me, you wouldn't have questions. Or doubts."

"I think you're talking in circles."

Wendy studied his handsome face for a few seconds, then pulled herself together. Even smiled. "No. I'm making perfect sense."

She was and because she was her common sense and strength returned. She loved Cullen enough to realize she'd never hold him. Never keep him. No one would. He was right. He was too scarred to trust enough to ever really fall in love.

She had to let him go. Freely. No regret. No remorse. He couldn't see any more tears. They couldn't have a sad goodbye on the twenty-third. He had to think she was totally okay with their situation.

She'd bear this hurt alone.

"And everything's okay."

Cullen pulled in a breath then said, "Are you sure?" as Harry turned from the trash can and headed over.

She forced a smile. "Everything's great."

Harry bounced over to them. Cullen rose and swung him over his shoulder. She saw all the love in him that he had to give, and knew with absolute certainty that he'd never give it. Not to her. Not to anyone. He'd always be alone.

And as much as she hurt for herself, she hurt more for him.

CHAPTER TWELVE

THE next morning, Wendy and Cullen didn't speak. He barricaded himself in his office and Wendy buried herself in her tasks for the day, aching with misery because she couldn't help herself, stop herself, from falling in love with a man who could never love her.

When the day was finally, mercifully, over, she hurried out of Barrington Candies and rushed home. Harry met her at the door of her house.

"Wendy! Wendy! I'm a star."

Her spirits lifted at the sight of him. She ruffled his hair. "I know you're a star."

"No, not that kind of star! I'm really a star! We're doing a play in the park the day before Christmas and I got picked to be the star. There are six sheep and three wise men, but only one star."

"So you really are a star?"

"Yes. Cullen's gonna love me!"

Her eyes welled with tears as she stooped down to his level. They'd been over this several times, and he never quite understood. "He's going home the day before Christmas Eve, remember?"

"Can't he stay one more day?"

She shook her head and appealed to Harry in a way he could understand. "His dad is all alone in Miami. If he doesn't go home, his dad doesn't have anybody to celebrate Christmas with."

Harry's happy face fell. "Oh."

"But you're still a star," she reminded him, praying that would take his mind off Cullen.

Harry's eyes instantly brightened. "That's right."

At work the next morning she immediately got down to business, keeping herself too busy to think of Cullen. At nine, he walked in, and, as if nothing were wrong, he said, "Good morning."

They were the first words he'd spoken to her since their disastrous night at the mall. She pulled in a breath and forced a smile, attempting to hide the dangerous hope that filled her heart. If he was talking, maybe they could make peace. Maybe she could talk him into staying the day to see Harry in the play.

"Good morning."

"How's Harry?"

"He's okay. He came home excited yesterday because he got a part in the Christmas play that's held every Christmas Eve in the park."

For that, he paused. "Oh, yeah?"

Pretending great interest in stacking the papers on her desk, desperately wanting to look like a normal assistant, so he wouldn't leave knowing he'd broken her heart, she said, "I think he'd love it if you'd stay long enough to see him."

She looked up just in time to see a shadow pass over his dark eyes. Had she not been holding his gaze, Wendy knew she would have missed it because it disappeared so quickly.

Turning to walk into his office, he said, "Sorry, I can't."

* * *

Cullen called the next morning, at six, according to the message he left on Wendy's office voice mail. He said he had everything caught up. There was no more work to be done. So he was going home early.

"Merry Christmas," he said, then he paused. He didn't speak for so long that Wendy was certain he'd hung up the phone, but he quietly added, "Tell Harry Merry Christmas, too. I wish I could have stayed for the play in the park."

The evening of December twenty-third found Cullen and his dad dressed in tuxedos, holding glasses of champagne, chatting with Mr. and Mrs. Chad Everly on their yacht.

Chad had been in real estate in New York City. Bonnie graced the cover of more magazines than any model before her. She was pretty and happy. Chad engaged Cullen's father in a discussion of futures that kept everybody on his conversational toes. And Cullen was bored.

He took a sip of champagne, glancing around at the models, actresses and career women, all dressed in glittering red, black, silver and gold dresses and couldn't help missing a woman in a simple red wool dress. If he closed his eyes, he could see her curly hair dancing around her shoulders, see the sparkle in her green eyes. If he focused he could even smell her perfume and remember the feeling of holding her while dancing.

"Cullen, you're a million miles away," Bonnie said, then wove her arm beneath Cullen's to slide him away from the serious conversation between her husband and his dad. "And there are at least twenty women here ready to vie for the position of your next lover."

He blinked. "What?"

She laughed. "Oh, come on. No one's so naive as to believe you'll ever take a wife."

He couldn't argue that.

"So everybody's happy to play the game." Bonnie paused by two tall, polished women. "I brought him."

Though this situation probably would have made him laugh the year before, he suddenly felt like a slab of beef. Confused by his sudden desire to look around for an escape route, he felt his cell phone vibrate in his pocket.

He smiled apologetically at the two women, reaching into his jacket pocket for the phone. "Sorry. For someone to call this late, it's got to be important."

As he walked away, he glanced at the caller ID and saw it was Wendy's number. But he didn't think it was her calling. He suspected it was Harry.

His heart twisted, but he didn't answer. There was no point in making things worse. He returned to the two women in sparkling diamonds and skin-tight holiday dresses, but suddenly thought again of Wendy's simple red dress. How not one of these women even came close to being as beautiful as she'd looked the night of Barrington Candy's Christmas party.

Annoyed with himself, he shook his head, tried to make conversation, and couldn't.

He returned to his father. "I think I might go home."

"What's the matter? Are you sick?"

"Tired."

"I told you Barrington Candies sucked people dry."

"The company's fine. I just want to be alone."

"You should see that place," his dad said, turning to the other people in their conversational circle. "It's a scrappy little town, full of people who will bleed you dry if you give them half a chance."

Cullen's mouth fell open, and he answered before he could stop himself. "That's not true!"

His dad chuckled. "When we get home, I'll show you the letters I've gotten over the past five years."

"You've gotten letters?"

"Whining about no raises."

"You told me you didn't know they hadn't gotten raises!"

"Cullen," he said, using his voice like a reprimand. "Do you really think I wasn't watching over the details of that company? Why do you think I knew the plant couldn't run itself while Paul was on vacation and I'd have to send you up to run it?"

"*You* told Paul McCoy not to give them raises?"

"It's a candy factory. Not rocket science. It doesn't require brains to work there. They were getting paid what they deserved until you started to like that little admin assistant and pitched a fit. I only authorized those raises so she wouldn't spend enough time trying to coerce you into giving raises that you'd do something you'd regret."

Cullen crossed his arms on his chest. "Like what, Dad?"

"Do you really want to get into this in front of your friends?"

"You mean *your* friends?"

"What has gotten into you?"

"Maybe I'm just starting to see the truth for the first time."

"Oh, come on! Get a drink. Enjoy yourself."

"Did you ever stop to think, Dad, that the reason Mom felt she had to work so hard for her friends was that she knew you were working against them?"

"Your mother knew exactly what she was getting when she married me."

"I don't think so."

He set his empty champagne glass on the tray of a passing waiter. "I'm going home."

"Wait!"

"No. I think I've waited long enough."

* * *

Wendy finally fell asleep around four, and slept until nine. Christmas Eve morning, she found Harry in the living room, curled up with Creamsicle, watching cartoons.

"Good morning."

"Hey, Wendy!" he said brightly, no worse for the wear over losing Cullen.

Ambling up the hall to her kitchen, she wished she could get over Cullen as easily as Harry had, then reminded herself that making wishes was part of why she was so miserable. Caught in her reverie, she nearly tripped over Creamsicle. His bell jingled merrily and he looked up at her accusingly.

"Hey, I'm sorry about the whole bell thing. But this was Cullen's choice. Not mine. Like a big dope, I fell in love just like you and Harry wanted. So I'm in the clear. And since there's nothing we can do about Cullen, you can scram. Go play with Harry."

She stepped over the fat cat and pushed open the kitchen door. Instead of heading back to the living room, Creamsicle followed her inside and leaped onto a stool beside the center island, his bell ringing again.

She swallowed. "You've got to stop with the bell." Tears filled her eyes. She understood Harry's desperation when he wished on bells. Because right now, right at this very second, she wished Cullen would walk through that door, tell her he'd made a mistake, tell her he loved her and wanted to be with her, and that they'd be together forever.

Turning away from Creamsicle, she shook her head. She couldn't mean that. She couldn't wish him back into her life. She was just emotional. She was too smart to wallow in misery or wish him back into her life.

But suddenly she remembered how happy he had been with the candy packers, what a great job he'd done running the factory, how happy he'd been at the Christmas party. When he'd arrived he'd been quiet and sullen. The factory and its workers had made him happy. *She'd* made him happy.

If his problem was fear of repeating his dad's mistakes when he couldn't see that their situation was totally different, then was it so wrong to wish for him to come back to the life he seemed to love?

No. He needed help.

She reached down and brushed Creamsicle's fur enough that the bell rang.

"I wish he would come back. I wish he would give us a chance. Even if he doesn't love me yet, I know he was falling." She brushed Creamsicle's fur again. The bell jingled. "I wish he would come back."

Her wish was forgotten in a haze of preparations for the play in the park. That night, Wendy stood shivering a few feet away from the gazebo "stage." Wanting to be supportive of Harry, she made sure she was visible so her little boy would know that his life was on track. Secure. He was hers. And she was here for him.

Rubbing her mitten-covered hands together, as she waited in the sea of parents and grandparents for the play to begin, she let her gaze ripple around the crowd. A flash of black leather stopped her heart.

Cullen.

He had a coat like that.

But as quickly as she thought she saw the swatch of coat, it disappeared.

Cullen raced into the park, searching for Wendy. The crowd unexpectedly parted and there she was. Standing to the right, twenty or so feet from the large stage-size gazebo where the children were performing, Wendy glowed with excitement.

His heart tripped over in his chest. The cold air had turned her cheeks a bright pink. Her eyes sparkled. The yellow scarf around her neck highlighted the cinnamon red of her hair. She was so beautiful, so happy, so alive, so real that he stood frozen. Why would she want him back when he'd hurt her? When he'd been confused over things that should have been obvious?

Harry Martin was an adorable star. Wendy could barely contain her happiness at his performance. As she jumped up and down, clapping for Harry, hands on her shoulders brought her back to the present, and she spun to see who was behind her.

"Boo."

"Boo?"

Cullen?

"You scared the devil out of me." And also stopped her heart. He looked amazing in his black leather jacket with the white wool scarf tied around his neck. There was just enough wind to ruffle his hair and color his cheeks. He looked so damned good she could have jumped into his arms. But she'd made that mistake at least twice already. Wouldn't make it again.

"Happy Christmas Eve." His words formed a white mist around him. A light snow began to fall. He lifted his face into it. "I'm so glad I'm home."

His referring to Barrington as home almost tripped her up, but she decided it must have been a slip of some sort. She refused to make anything of it.

"Did you come back to see Harry in the play?"

"Yes. And wasn't he funny? I've never seen a kid happier to be a star. But I also came back because Tom Ross couldn't take the job after all. When he put in his notice, his employer doubled his salary." He pulled in a breath. "So, Barrington Candies lost him."

Not knowing what else to say, she said simply, "That's too bad."

"Not really. I want the job."

She stifled the urge to squeeze her eyes shut in misery. She couldn't work with him, knowing he didn't love her—*couldn't* love her—when she was head over heels in love with him.

"Yep. I'm going to take over the company and keep my dad out of it."

The tone of his voice hinted that there was a story behind that decision and Wendy itched with curiosity. But she said nothing.

"Yeah. And with it being Christmas Eve my hotel's booked. So it looks like I'll be staying with you tonight."

"Not on your life." That broke her vow of silence. "There's no ice storm. And don't you dare mention this to Harry. He won't understand why I can't let you stay and he'll be upset with me, when you're the culprit."

He put his finger over her lips to silence her. "Not really. I got my priorities straightened out really quickly on a yacht last night, and I had a little something made for you." He produced a ring box from his jacket pocket and handed it to her. "Open it."

She swallowed hard. Her heart pounding in her chest, she forced her trembling fingers to open the box. A brilliant diamond winked at her.

"Will you marry me?"

Her eyes widened in shock and she gaped at Cullen. "Marry you? You leave me one day, and two days later you come back and ask me to marry you?"

"I know the timing seems a bit quick. But I think I fell in love with you the night I stayed at your house and toasted marshmallows. Unless I miss my mark, you love me, too. So I really can't see a reason to wait. Especially when we have Harry to consider. God only knows what he'd tell his teacher if I spent too many nights before we made it official."

She laughed through her tears. "I thought you didn't believe in marriage."

Taking the ring box from her hand, he said, "I've had some revelations in the past twenty-four hours." He slid the ring out and slipped it on her finger. "My dad spent his adult life telling me love never lasted. But I think what he was really saying was that *his* love hadn't lasted. I think ours will."

She looked down at the sparkling ring. "I know ours will."

"You're sure enough to put up with me every day for the next fifty or sixty years?"

She laughed. "It will be my pleasure."

"Then it looks like we're getting married."

Harry skipped over. "Hey, Cullen!"

"Hey, kid."

"I knew you'd come."

Cullen laughed and ruffled Harry's hair. "Why? Did you wish on a bell again?"

"No, Wendy did."

Cullen threw his head back and laughed.

"Harry, you and I are going to have to work on your secret-keeping abilities."

Harry just grinned.

"Doesn't matter," Cullen said, sliding his arm around Wendy's waist as he took Harry's hand.

Harry looked up at him. "It doesn't?"

"Nope, Wendy and I are going to get married. None of us will be keeping secrets anymore."

The church bells began to chime out the hour, and Cullen leaned over and kissed Wendy.

Harry grinned. There were some things about adults he would never understand, but he did understand the power of wishes. He raised his eyes to the sky and whispered, "Thanks."

Cullen pulled away from Wendy and caught her hand. "Let's go home."

Harry had never heard better words.

EPILOGUE

CARRYING a tray holding three servings of scrambled eggs and toast, Cullen led Harry up the stairs on Christmas morning.

"Can I give her my present first?"

"Yes," Cullen answered, dropping his voice to a whisper. "But keep your voice down or she'll know we're coming. It won't be a surprise."

Harry stage-whispered, "Okay."

Stifling a laugh, Cullen finished the climb up the stairs and walked to the bedroom he'd shared with Wendy the night before. When she fell asleep, he'd been so overcome with love that he'd slipped out of bed and awakened Harry.

Neither one of them had bought Wendy a Christmas gift. After one phone call to the jeweler who'd made her engagement ring, banking on his festive goodwill and promising him it would be a large purchase, he and Harry had bounded out into the night.

As he stepped into the bedroom, Harry raced past him and bounced on the bed. "Get up! It's Christmas."

Wendy stirred.

"Really, Wendy, get up! I have a present for you and Santa left presents for me and I want to open them."

Cullen set the tray across her knees. "You don't want breakfast first?"

Harry peered at Cullen over his glasses. "No."

Wendy sat up. "You're at least having toast."

Cullen bent across the tray and kissed Wendy. "Good morning."

She smiled. "Good morning."

Harry bounced across the bed to kneel beside her. He grabbed a piece of toast. Before stuffing most of it into his mouth he said, "Open mine first."

"I think I'd rather have coffee first."

Harry's face fell comically. "But I want to open my presents."

Wendy laughed and relented. "I was teasing." She ruffled his soft yellow hair. "So what do you have for me?"

He thrust the small package at her. "You're gonna love it."

"I'm sure I will," she said, ripping off the paper. When she saw the logo on the elegant box, she glanced over at Cullen. "How did he get something from Smithmeyers?"

Cullen shrugged. "I don't know. Maybe Santa took him."

Harry giggled.

"You snuck out in the middle of the night, didn't you?"

Cullen shook his head, looking as innocent as a newborn babe. Harry giggled merrily.

Wendy glanced from one to the other, then pulled the lid off the box to reveal a sterling-silver Christmas-tree ornament, engraved with the words *Our First Christmas as a Family* and the year.

Tears blurred Wendy's vision. "It's beautiful." She reached out and hugged Harry. "Perfect."

Cullen pulled a long, thin box from his trouser pocket. "Well, since you're already crying, here's mine."

She took the little box that was all but hidden by curled

ribbons and opened it. A diamond necklace caught the morning light streaming in through her bay window and winked at her.

"Oh, my gosh!" She looked up at Cullen. "You do know I have nowhere to wear this, right?"

He laughed. "I have a home in Miami, lots of friends in New York."

She swallowed. "I'm…I'm…"

Obviously seeing his opportunity, Harry filled in the blank, saying, "Ready to go downstairs so I can open my presents?"

Wendy laughed through her tears. "Okay. You go ahead downstairs, Harry. Cullen and I will be down in a minute."

Harry sighed. "Okay, but don't kiss too long."

The second Harry was out of earshot, Cullen said, "We may live and work in Barrington, but I'd like to show you the world."

She looked up at him. They'd talked and talked the night before, listened to each other's hopes, learned each other's dreams. So she knew this was important to him. "I'd like to see the world."

"Good." He kissed her, then rose from the bed. "We'd better get down to the living room before Harry starts making wishes on Creamsicle's bell again."

Wendy laughed and tossed back the covers. "Heaven only knows what he'd wish for now."

Catching her hand, Cullen led her from the bedroom. "Probably brothers and sisters."

As he said the words, Cullen stopped. Turning to face Wendy, he grinned as if something miraculous had just occurred to him. "We could have kids."

"As many as you want."

His grin grew. "This is going to be fun."

"Greatest adventure ever."

With that they left the bedroom, raced down the stairs and watched Harry open more presents than Wendy had ever seen under a tree.

She would never be alone again.

Neither would Cullen.

And neither would Harry.

CHRISTMAS TREATS

For an early Christmas present Susan Meier would like to
share a little treat with you...

"I got the idea for Harry's cookie-painting fun from my
mother, Helen Petrunak. Every Friday after Thanksgiving,
rather than battle shoppers, she hosts a 'cookie-painting party'
for her grandkids.

"She bakes sugar cookies and the kids paint them with
colorful icing. They paint faces on Santa cookies, stained-glass
windows on church cookies and red noses on reindeer cookies.

"When dry, the cookies are hung on a Christmas tree in the
family room. The 'goodie' tree is decorated with cookies,
bubble gum and candy canes. The kids wait eagerly for the
day they can plunder the goodies hanging from the bright-
green limbs."

CHRISTMAS CUT-OUT COOKIES

1 cup butter, softened
1 cup sugar
1 egg
2 tbsp orange juice
1 tbsp vanilla
2 ½ cups all-purpose flour
1 tsp baking powder

Combine butter, sugar and egg in large bowl. Beat with mixer on medium speed, scraping bowl often, until creamy. Add orange juice and vanilla; mix well. In a separate bowl, sift together flour and baking powder. Add flour and baking powder mixture to sugar, butter and egg mixture in easily blended increments, mixing with mixer on low speed. Beat until well blended.

Divide the dough into thirds; wrap in plastic wrap. Refrigerate until firm (two to three hours). When dough is firm, heat oven to 400°F. Remove one-third of dough from refrigerator. On lightly floured surface, roll out to ⅛" to ¼" thickness. (Keep remaining dough refrigerated.) Cut with 3-inch cookie cutters. Place 1 inch apart on ungreased cookie sheets.*

Bake 6 to 10 minutes or until edges are lightly browned; cool completely. "Paint" with colorful icing.

* If you're using the cookies for decorations and need a way to hang them, a drinking straw will cut a perfect hole for hanging. After cookies are placed on cookie sheet, cut a hole

in the top of each cookie using a drinking straw. Press the straw into the dough, leaving approximately 1/4 inch of dough around the hole. Bake as above and cool. After the cookies are painted, run ribbon through the hole and tie in a bow to create a loop to hang the cookie on the tree.

GRANDMA'S SHINY ICING FOR COOKIES

2 egg whites
1 tbsp lemon juice
1 to 1 ½ cups powdered sugar
(extra ½ cup only used as needed)
Food coloring

Mix egg whites, lemon juice and most of the cup of powdered sugar. If the mixture is too thin, continue to add the remainder of the first cup of powdered sugar in increments until you have a consistency of icing that can be spread or painted onto the cookies. If it is still too thin after an entire cup of powdered sugar, add increments of the extra powdered sugar until you get the correct consistency. It can't be too thick or too thin. If it's too thick, add a few drops of water.

Separate the icing into several small bowls. Dye the icing in each of the bowls using enough food coloring to create the colors you desire. Icing can be spread on cookies, or painted on with a thin brush, depending on how fancy you intend to make your cookies.

Celebrate 60 years of pure reading pleasure
with Harlequin®!
Just in time for the holidays,
Silhouette Special Edition® is proud to present
New York Times *bestselling author*
Kathleen Eagle's
ONE COWBOY, ONE CHRISTMAS

Rodeo rider Zach Beaudry was a travelin' man—until he
broke down in middle-of-nowhere South Dakota during
a deep freeze. That's when an angel came to his rescue....

"Don't die on me. Come on, Zel. You know how much I love you, girl. You're all I've got. Don't do this to me here. Not *now*."

But Zelda had quit on him, and Zach Beaudry had no one to blame but himself. He'd taken his sweet time hitting the road, and then miscalculated a shortcut. For all he knew he was a hundred miles from gas. But even if they were sitting next to a pump, the ten dollars he had in his pocket wouldn't get him out of South Dakota, which was not where he wanted to be right now. Not even his beloved pickup truck, Zelda, could get him much of anywhere on fumes. He was sitting out in the cold in the middle of nowhere. And getting colder.

He shifted the pickup into Neutral and pulled hard on the steering wheel, using the downhill slope to get her off the blacktop and into the roadside grass, where she shuddered to a standstill. He stroked the padded dash. "You'll be safe here."

But Zach would not. It was getting dark, and it was already too damn cold for his cowboy ass. Zach's battered body was a barometer, and he was feeling South Dakota, big time. He'd have given his right arm to be climbing into a hotel hot tub instead of a brutal blast of north wind. The right was his free arm anyway. Damn thing had lost altitude, touched some part of the bull and caused him a scoreless ride last time out.

It wasn't scoring him a ride this night, either. A carload of teenagers whizzed by, topping off the insult by laying on the horn as they passed him. It was at least twenty minutes before another vehicle came along. He stepped out and waved both arms this time, damn near getting himself killed. Whatever happened to *do unto others?* In places like this, decent people didn't leave each other stranded in the cold.

His face was feeling stiff, and he figured he'd better start walking before his toes went numb. He struck out for a distant yard light, the only sign of human habitation in sight. He couldn't tell how distant, but he knew he'd be hurting by the time he got there, and he was counting on some kindly old man to be answering the door. No shame among the lame.

It wasn't like Zach was fresh off the operating table—it had been a few months since his last round of repairs—but he hadn't given himself enough time. He'd lopped a couple of weeks off the near end of the doc's estimated recovery time, rigged up a brace, done some heavy-duty taping and climbed onto another bull. Hung in there for five seconds—four seconds past feeling the pop in his hip and three seconds short of the buzzer.

He could still feel the pain shooting down his leg with every step. Only this time he had to pick the damn thing up, swing it forward and drop it down again on his own.

Pride be damned, he just hoped *somebody* would be answering the door at the end of the road. The light in the front window was a good sign.

The four steps to the covered porch might as well have been four hundred, and he was looking to climb them with a lead weight chained to his left leg. His eyes were just as screwed up as his hip. Big black spots danced around with tiny red flashers, and he couldn't tell what was real and what wasn't. He stumbled over some shrubbery, steadied himself on the porch railing and peered between vertical slats.

There in the front window stood a spruce tree with a silver star affixed to the top. Zach was pretty sure the red sparks were all in his head, but the white lights twinkling by the hundreds throughout the huge tree, those were real. He wasn't too sure about the woman hanging the shiny balls. Most of her hair was caught up on her head and fastened in a curly clump, but the light captured by the escaped bits crowned her with a golden halo. Her face was a soft shadow, her body a willowy silhouette beneath a long white gown. If this was where the mind ran off to when cold started shutting down the rest of the body, then Zach's final worldly thought was, *This ain't such a bad way to go.*

If she would just turn to the window, he could die looking into the eyes of a Christmas angel.

* * * * *

Could this woman from Zach's past get the lonesome
cowboy to come in from the cold...for good?
Look for
ONE COWBOY, ONE CHRISTMAS
by Kathleen Eagle
Available December 2009
from Silhouette Special Edition®

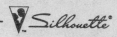

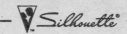

SPECIAL EDITION

**FROM *NEW YORK TIMES* AND *USA TODAY*
BESTSELLING AUTHOR**

KATHLEEN EAGLE

ONE COWBOY,
One Christmas

When bull rider Zach Beaudry appeared
out of thin air on Ann Drexler's ranch,
she thought she was seeing a ghost of
Christmas past. And though Zach had
no memory of their night of passion years
ago, they were about to share a future
he would never forget.

*Available December 2009
wherever books are sold.*

SSE65493